USA TODAY BESTSELLING AUTHOR

SKYE MACKINNON

BOOK TWO

DAUGHTER OF WINTER

WINTER HEIRESS

PERYTON PRESS

Contents

Daughter of Winter series   9
What Happened Before   11

Chapter 1   15
Chapter 2   23
Chapter 3   37
Chapter 4   53
Chapter 5   73
Chapter 6   91
Chapter 7   107
Chapter 8   119
Chapter 9   137
Chapter 10   147
Chapter 11   159
Chapter 12   171
Chapter 13   187
Chapter 14   201
Chapter 15   215
Epilogue   221

Author's Note   225
About the Author   226
Also by Skye MacKinnon   227

*To all the teachers who tried to talk me out of following my
dreams.
Take this, bitches.*

Daughter of Winter series

Winter Princess

Winter Heiress

Winter Queen

Winter Goddess

\>> Box set

Mother of Gods (prequel)

Demon's Revenge (spin-off)

Samhain Goddess (sequel)

Set in the same world:

Guardians of Winter

What Happened Before

As a demi-goddess, Wyn has always stood out from the human crowd. On her 22nd birthday, her magic finally surfaces and she almost levels her street. Luckily, four Guardians arrive just on time: The mysterious and occasionally grumpy Storm, his cheery twin brother Frost, kilt-wearing Arc and funny, gentle Crispin.

They've been sent by Wyn's mother, a Goddess, to bring her to the the Winter Realm, but Wyn has enemies, even if she doesn't know it yet...

After failed kidnapping and assassination attempts (and a bit of kissing), the five reach the Standing Stones at Calanais which are the Gate to the Winter Realm. Unfortunately, an army of demons awaits them there.

Wyn doesn't have much control over her new magic yet, so she gets one training session with each of the Guardians. They stay the night with demoness Chesca and her Guardian lover Aodh.

The next day, the battle begins. Wyn and her Guardians win, but Aodh gets killed in the process and Wyn loses access to her magic. They have some rainbow sex before arriving in the Winter Realm, where they're frostily welcomed by Beira.

However, Wyn soon learns that it's all been an act and that her mother really loves her. When Beira is almost killed by an assassin sent by the Summer King, Angus, Wyn manages to save her and unlocks her magic in the process.

The books ends with Beira admitting that she is getting weaker and that she will need Wyn's help to fight Angus.

Chapter One

"Crispin! If you don't come here this very moment, I'm going to turn you into the ugliest icicle this Realm has ever seen!"

I've learned to add 'ugly' to any threat – he'd never admit it, but he's the vainest of all my Guardians.

"What has he done now?" Tamara asks, looking up from the book she's reading. She was one of the first to notice that I'm not at all like my mother, and she's taking full advantage of it. Whenever she has some free time - which is not very often - she spends it in my warm sitting room, reading by the fire. It's nice to have some female company from time to time, even though she could be my grandmother. I've not found the courage yet to ask her about her age. She may be small and old, but she's fierce and a little scary. It didn't take me long to figure out that she's the person who pulls all the strings in the palace. All the generals with their medals are only her puppets, nothing more.

"Are you having a little lovers' quarrel?"

Her eyes twinkle in delight. She loves a good gossiping.

"Look what he did to my dress for tonight!" I throw her the garment and she catches it with one hand. Good reflexes for her age, that's for sure.

Mara unfolds the dress and starts to giggle.

"I like that boy. He's got a good sense of humour."

I sigh in exasperation. "He cut holes into my dress. Two holes in two very inappropriate places. I wouldn't call that humour. It's malicious mischief."

That only increased Mara's laughter. "I hope you're going to wear it like that to the ball?"

"No chance."

"Then you're giving him what he wants. Show him that you stand above his jokes. Wear the dress, but with a few modifications." She gives me a wink and leads me to the wardrobe.

May my revenge be sweet.

I've lost count of the number of balls my mother is organising in my honour. They're all aimed at different audiences: The Guardians, the common folk, the military, the diplomatic community. Now that she has recovered from her assassination attempt, she's hellbent on showing everyone that nothing has changed. That she's still the Queen and Mother of Gods and just as strong as ever. And it seems to work; the rumours that floated through the palace for a few days after the attack have quieted down. I'm glad for Beira - even though it's not true. She's getting weaker and she's refusing to tell me why. She's very adept at keeping up appearances, but when we're alone in our private quarters, she sometimes lets down the walls she's built.

The assassination attempt has left her weakened, but it's not just that. Her magic isn't as strong as it used to be, and that's never happened before. I think deep down she's scared, and to be honest, so am I. I've known her as this unapproachable, divine being for all my life, and to think that she's got weaknesses boggles my mind. It makes her more human, sure, but she's not supposed to be human.

"Please stand for the Daughter of Winter, the Slayer of Demons, the Heir to the Throne, her Royal Highness, the Lady Wynter."

Slayer of Demons, that's a new one. I assume it's been one of the guys who told the herald to say that. They like to do stuff like that. I think they're a little bored and messing with the Court routine gives them a bit of satisfaction.

I enter the Great Hall to the sound of applause and am tempted to leave immediately. I hate the attention I get at these kinds of events. It's bad enough having to sit still at the dais, surrounded by the most important people in the Realm. Doing small talk. Bleurgh. But walking through the biggest room in the palace, trying not to trip or look awkward on my way to the other end is pure torture. And tonight, I don't even have my Guardians to steady me. They're in some kind of meeting and won't be joining us until later.

Now that they've safely brought me to my mother's domain, they've started taking on some of their old tasks again. They're still my assigned guards, but having four of them around me at all times would be a waste of resources. They're some of the best fighters in the Realm, after all, and they're in high demand to pass on their skills to the younger Guardians. I'm not quite sure how I feel about that. On one hand, I'm glad I don't have an entourage wherever I go, on the other hand, I miss having them around all the time. Even at night, it's rarely all of us together. Storm is the one who's absent the most, being the highest ranking of the four. Sometimes he's away all night and then sleeps in the morning when I have my own things to do.

I miss our days on the road. It was stressful, dangerous, but I loved it. Now, we're in stasis, surrounded by Court formality and intrigue, always the subject of gossip. I'm slowly learning how to behave in this setting, but I make enough mistakes to entertain the servants.

Another thing I can't get used to: servants. They learned pretty quickly that I prefer to take a bath on my own, thank you very much. If I want company, I'll take one (or several) of my Guardians with me. I don't need handmaidens messing with my hair or handing me clothes, and I absolutely can't stand them telling me how beautiful I am when they apply my makeup. Whenever I look into a mirror, I don't recognise myself. My features have changed, my cheekbones are higher, my eyes brighter, my hair glossier. I'm no longer plain and ordinary and I'm hating it. I want to go back to being the old Wyn, the one who could put her hair into a messy bun and stay in pyjamas all day long while working on her thesis. Here, I have to wear pretty dresses and behave like a lady. Yuck.

"Walk," the herald hisses and I notice I'm standing in the large doorway, being stared at by the hundreds of guests waiting for me to make my way to the dais. Luckily, my mother hasn't arrived yet. Despite our differences, I do seek her approval. She's the expert in how to be Queen, so I better learn from her how to behave like a princess.

Ignoring the stares and hushed conversations, I walk through the Hall, keeping my eyes trained on the high table. Out of the corner of my eyes, I see a few people pointing at my chest. I'm sure Mara will give me a roundup of public opinion later on. I'm either setting a new trend or making myself the laughing stock of the Court.

Instead of having my boobs on display like Crispin intended when he cut two holes into my dress, I now have a strip of ruffled black fabric running around my upper body like a corset that's too high, culminating in a large golden bow on my chest. The holes are used for the golden band to disappear back into the dress, giving it a three-dimensional appearance. It's crazy. And I have to admit that I quite like the effect. It makes me look like a Christmas present that is waiting to be unwrapped. Not now; later, after the feast, by my four Guardians. Who will hopefully be here soon, so I can tease them all evening.

This is the first time I make it to my seat without stumbling. I may turn into a proper princess yet. As soon as I sit down, the guests follow suit and start their conversations once more. A few are still looking in my direction, but most are finally distracted again. None of the other important guests have arrived yet, so I sit on my own, letting my thoughts drift. I've been here for two weeks now and it feels both shorter and longer at the same time. There's so much to learn and so much to understand that I sometimes think my head will explode. Some of the Court rules are archaic and desperately need some modernisation. The lack of electronics is still strange, but at the same time, their magic makes many things possible that technology never would. Who needs Skype when you can have a telepathic conversation?

The air here is filled with magic and my very own magic is responding to it. She gets stronger every day - and a little wilder. Sometimes she's hard to control, it's as if she gets high on magical energy. The Guardians told me that it would become easier to control her over time, but somehow, I'm experiencing the opposite. Most days, I'm having to fight to keep her inside. She's like a kitten that wants to play with a ball of string even though she knows its forbidden.

Yesterday, I accidentally froze my bathwater. Luckily, nobody else was in the room with me so I was saved from the embarrassment. But I'm a little scared at how easily my magic dispelled my hold on her and ran amok.

"How are you tonight, darling?" my mother suddenly asks as she materialises next to me. I envy that skill, it would have saved me from walking through the hall like an idiot. Or like a princess, which was basically the same thing. I really wasn't cut out to be royalty.

"I'm alright," I reply vaguely and turn my attention to the food that had magically appeared on the plate in front of me. I was still getting used to all the magic here. Back on Earth, I had to hide my abilities. Here, I'm more than just encouraged to use them; it's expected of me. The ladies at Court don't use their hands for most things, they use their magic. Brushing your hair? Use magic. Apply makeup? Use magic. Wipe your bum? You get the idea...

"What are you having for dinner?" Beira asks me. Is she attempting small talk or is she actually interested? I glance at my plate. Pancakes, strawberries and a heap of cream. Comfort food. I must be feeling like I'm in need of a hug. Or four.

"Do you need me for anything tomorrow?" I ask her instead. "I'd like to go and explore the area a little."

"You want to... Why not? I guess you should know the Realm you're ruling over. But not without your Guardians."

That was exactly what I was hoping for. This means I get them all for myself, for an entire day. No politics, no boring stuff, just me and my four men. It will be just like being back on the road. Hopefully with a bit less danger.

Speaking of the devils... Crispin and Frost enter together, mostly ignored by the crowd who're busy emptying their plates. They spot me immediately – the disadvantage of sitting on the dais in full view of everyone. I give them a wave and smile, but they continue to stare at me from a distance. Crispin is pointing at me – no, at my boobs. That's when I remember my dress and I grin mischievously. He's noticed how I turned the joke on him. Poor Guardian. He looks like a sad little puppy who's had his favourite toy taken away. That's the punishment for cutting up my clothes.

"By the way, I love your dress, darling," my mother says at that moment and I snort loudly, totally unbefitting a Princess.

Chapter Two

"Are you sure you'll be able to fly the whole way?" Storm asks me carefully. It's clear that he'd rather have me take the portable throne again. No chance. I'll never get into that contraption again. Especially not now that I have wings. Beautiful, shimmering, almost translucent wings. I flutter them slightly and watch as they reflect the light in all colours of the rainbow. I'm still not entirely used to the feeling, but I've definitely fallen in love with how they look. People on Earth would probably think that I'm a fairy. If only they knew.

"I'll manage," I respond in my Princess voice, the one that doesn't allow any arguments. It's rare that I'm pulling rank, but today I really want to fly. And if I fall, I'm sure one of my four Guardians will catch me. If not... oh well, it'll work out somehow.

"Your Highness, I've prepared you a picnic." Tamara comes hurrying up the stairs to the top of the tower where we're waiting to begin our trip. So far, I've not managed to launch into the air from the ground. Luckily, my mother's palace has a multitude of towers at my disposal.

"Thank you, Mara." I smile at her and take the basket she's brought us. I never thought I'd have a picnic in winter, but why not. It's always winter here in the Realm, so I better get used to it. Most people use their magic to stay warm; otherwise the ladies at court would never be able to wear their flimsy dresses. They all seem to think that nakedness is fashionable. I shudder. No, I prefer to be dressed properly.

I pass the basket on to Crispin - I'm not sure if I could carry the extra weight with my untrained wings - and give the boys a grin. "Ready?"

Before they can respond, I jump off the tower.

Falling.

Falling.

How do I move my wings again?

Ah. Flying!

Just before I hit the ground, my wings fully expand and I glide in an elegant curve over the frosty fields that surround the palace on this side. With a few beats of my wings, I ascend. Above me, my men are waiting for me. Their perfect movements show me what I still have to learn. And I will, in time. They've had years to practice flying. I've only had two weeks.

Flying is exhilarating. The wind tousles my hair as I fly higher to join them. My magic is keeping me in a cocoon of warm air, immediately melting the tiny snowflakes that have started falling from the clouds above us. Not the perfect weather for a picnic.

They all look at me in disapproval, but I ignore them. "So, where are we going?" I ask cheerily. Just because this was my idea doesn't mean I actually know where to go. All I've seen of the Realm so far is the Gate and the palace, and the bits in between. But after looking at some of the maps, I could spend years exploring my new home. And if my mother gets what she wants, I might do just that.

She wants me to stay forever, basically. I'm not sure I like that idea. My parents still live on Earth - my adoptive parents, that is, but they raised me and I know them a lot better than Beira. And I never finished my studies... I had a life back there and I don't want to give it all up. While this Princess-experience is quite a lot of fun at the moment, it's also terribly boring in the long run. I'll never get used to having servants and living in a massive palace that is basically a town in itself.

But right now, my mother needs me. Once her strength returns... we will see.

"We'll head West," Storm announces and starts to fly off, leaving the rest of us to follow.

"Why is he being grumpy?" I ask Frost, who's flying next to me.

"He doesn't think this is a good idea. There have been reports of Summer soldiers in the Realms, and he is worried that we might encounter some."

"Summer soldiers, here? Why didn't I know that?"

He looks a bit uncomfortable. "It's not common knowledge."

I huff. "Well, I'm not exactly common. Shouldn't the heiress to the Winter throne know such things?"

"Yer mother didnae want ta worry ya." Arc appears on my other side, the tip of his wings almost touching mine.

My good mood is quickly disappearing. "She keeps saying she wants me to take over some of her duties. How am I supposed to do that if she doesn't tell me what's going on?"

"She was waiting ta find oot if they're here for ye," Arc says. My head is spinning. This all doesn't make any sense.

"Why would they be here for me? I was told the Summer King wanted to prevent me from reaching my mother, but I'm here now, so why would he want to go after me? He's failed and I'm now under Beira's protection. Surely he's got no chance of actually getting close to the palace?"

"We've got some theories, but until any of them have been proven, let's not talk about it," Storm growls from the front, his deep voice carrying despite the wind getting stronger.

"No way!" I shout back. "I want answers, now!"

Frost clears his throat. "Wyn, you're sparking."

"What?" I look down at myself and notice a plume of smoke trailing me. Oops. What has my magic done now?

I check on her and find her running around in circles, colourful sparks flying all around her. What the hell?

"Bad girl," I tell her and she looks at me, grinning widely. She's been really badly behaved recently. Maybe she's going through puberty? It's getting harder to control her, especially now that she's getting stronger. All the magic here must be messing with her understanding of the rules. And one of those rules is not to set me on fire.

"Sit in a corner," I command but all she does is show me her pink tongue. Maybe I should talk to my mother about this. Or one of the Guardians, although they all think it's crazy that I talk to my magic. That I see her as a distinct entity. So maybe not, they wouldn't know what to do.

"I think we need to give you some lessons," Frost says with a smirk and I perk up. Is he talking about... no, he means my magic. Pity. I've not had as much physical contact with them as I would like. I thought once we'd get to the palace and have a life where we weren't running from assassins and fighting demons, we'd have more alone time. But no, everybody's so busy that I'm rarely alone with all of them. I could probably count the times all five of us have sat together on one hand.

I should really enjoy this trip and leave the questions for later. I will get my answers though, even if I have to invent new torture methods. Maybe if I play all innocent now, they'll forget our argument and will be more easily convinced to part with their knowledge later? A girl can hope...

I send some water magic over my back to extinguish any sparks that may still be lingering there. I'm amazed I haven't actually burned myself. That would be so like me. A whoosh of warm air dries my clothes immediately. Magic does come in handy.

We fly in silence, although Frost shoots me a smile from time to time. He's not going to let the almost-burning-myself-by-accident go anytime soon. Well, I've got enough dirt on him to retaliate.

"We're almost there!" Storm shouts from the front. "Will you manage to land?"

I cringe at his doubts in my skills - but they are well-founded. I try and move the memory of crashing into one of the palace towers out of my mind. I've still got bruises on my bum. Flying is hard, but landing is even harder. And painful, in most of my attempts so far. Let's hope this time will be more graceful. I've got four guys watching me, after all, and despite being their Princess I still want to impress them. Don't ask me why, my brain is weird.

"Yes!" I reply loudly, trying to sound confident. Maybe if they believe in me, it will work?

"Don't forget to use your wind magic to buffer your fall," Crispin whispers from behind and I give him a grateful nod. Always good to have a plan B. Combining different kinds of magic is one thing I'm still struggling with. And using magic while flying... not easy. But then I remember how I instinctively extinguished the sparks and warmed my clothes after, and smile. Looks like I'm making progress, even if I'm not noticing it immediately.

We descend towards a solitary pine tree in a vast expanse of ice. There's nothing here but frozen ground. No houses, no people, only this one tree. Having grown up in a city, this is very alien to me. Even when we went on trips into the hills, there were always other people around. Not here, though. Nothing grows in these plains, and there is no reason for anybody to be here. Except for us. I have no idea why Storm chose this as the place for our picnic.

Storm accelerates and lands on the ice below us. Maybe he wants to catch me if I fall. I'm not sure if I feel insulted or cared for. These men are messing with my feelings again. Having one boyfriend was hard enough back on Earth - it lasted about two months before he gave up on me - but now I have four. There should be handbook for this. How to have your own male harem. Or: How to cope with four times the normal testosterone.

They're driving me crazy. But then, they probably think the

same thing about me. I know I'm not the easiest person to be around. Or the most stable.

I adjust the angle of my wings just like the guys showed me. Theoretically, this should enable a smooth landing. I reach for my wind magic and create a pillow of air hovering above the ground. Just in case. I don't want to ruin this picnic by breaking anything.

"Go for it," Frost cheers me on and I dip my wings, going into the final dive down.

Ten seconds later, I'm very thankful for the air cushion I created. I'm lying on it, three feet off the snowy ground, nursing my bruised ego. I probably looked like a dodo falling from the sky. With even worse wing coordination.

All four of the guys have landed and are watching me, in various stages of hiding their laughter. Or in Crispin's case, not hiding it at all. He's bent over laughing. I growl at him. He's insulting my ailing dignity.

I deflate my magic pillow and am gently lowered to the ground. Now that's what my landing should have looked like. Arc comes over and puts an arm around my shoulders.

"Dinnae worry, lass. It takes some time ta learn how ta fly."

"I know how to fly," I protest. "Just not how to land."

Crispin is shaken by another fit of giggles. That man has no respect for his Princess.

To change the topic, I ask, "Why are we here? What's so special about this place?"

Storm gives me a rare smile. "Use your magic to find out."

I frown but do as he says. I expand my senses, reaching out for any signs of magical activity. There's a slight humming beneath the ground that I focus on. I'm hesitant to use my Earth magic, as it seems to be the one I have least control over, but I send a tendril of magic into the ground, feeling for anything unusual.

The humming increases the further I reach. Something is hidden in the Earth, something big. There's a point to my right that calls to me, and without thinking, I walk to it and stop only a few feet away from the tree. It's beneath me, whatever it is.

I look to the guys for guidance and Storm nods. Looks like I'm doing the right thing. I send a bit more magic into the ground, feeding that strange point that is attracting me. It feels like an orb that's been buried beneath the surface. And it needs to be filled to... to do what exactly?

The guys would have told me if this was dangerous, right? They wouldn't let me feed magic to a monster that will eat us any second now? No, they're sensible, most of the time. I send the final bit of magic into it - and the ground begins to shake.

"What's happening?" I ask, slightly panicked. I remember the first time I made the ground shake, when the guys had to subdue me before I levelled the street.

"Wait and see," Crispin grins, staring at the tree in expectation.

The tree looks just the same - no, wait, it's slowly starting to twist. Its thin trunk pirouettes gracefully before the entire tree jumps to one side, leaving a hole in the ground.

"What. The. Fuck." I stare at the tree which is now in a new place, looking as if it's been growing there all its life. "What just happened?"

"So impatient," Frost chuckles. "As Crisp said: wait and see."

It's not in my nature to be patient, but with the guys not budging, I have no choice. I look at the hole, carefully approaching it. It's just about wide enough to let someone big like Arc squeeze through. I shoot him a glance. His muscles... yummy.... no, Wyn, you're not looking at his muscles, you're looking at his circumference. Yes, he should fit.

Nothing happens.

"Do we have to jump in?" I ask and turn to look at them - and swirl around a second later as a loud bang signals that something is happening.

"Aww, ye missed it," Arc says. I huff in disappointment but then he chuckles. "Just kidding. Watch now."

This time, I don't turn but stare at the hole, trying not to blink. A faint pink mist starts to rise from the ground. No, not pink, rainbow coloured. Just like on my wings, hundreds of colours swirl into each other, creating the illusion of a rainbow. It's beautiful. The mist begins to solidify and form a shape, almost as tall as me.

"Is that a horse?" I ask, but the guys shush me.

"Do not use the word 'horse' during the next few hours," Storm warns me. "Our host is allergic to it."

"What?" I ask in confusion, but all they do is groan. Really, they should be used to me asking questions by now. When I first met them, Crispin said he found it endearing. Now I'm not so sure. He's probably changed his mind. Gods, even I know I can be annoying.

The mist swirls faster, getting ever more solid, until it suddenly turns white. And it's the shape of a....

"A unicorn?" I ask open-mouthed. "But unicorns don't exist."

"Don't they?" the unicorn replies drily, and I think I'm about to faint. It's a real-life unicorn. I repeat, a UNICORN. Like a white horse (oops!) but with an ivory coloured horn that looks like it could easily kill a few demons. Its fur is shimmering with a hint of rainbow and its hooves are bright silver.

"Am I hallucinating?" I ask weakly and the guys laugh. Those evil Guardians could have warned me.

"You didn't get this weird when you saw you had wings," Crispin remarks and I'm tempted to set him on fire. On purpose, not like my usual accidents.

"But it's a unicorn..." I mumble, aware that I'm not making much sense. I've loved unicorns ever since I was little. When I found out that Scotland's national animal is a unicorn, I was the happiest girl on the planet. Scotland is full of unicorn statues and coat of arms. Take Stirling Castle for example, they even have giant tapestries depicting a unicorn which is being captured by a virgin. Oh.

"So the legend of needing a maiden to attract a unicorn isn't true?" I ask my Guardians, fully aware that they've found out by themselves that I wasn't a virgin. And after our... bedroom adventures, I'd definitely not be one anymore.

"No, but any maiden is welcome to appear to me," the unicorn cackles. I don't think my eyes can get any wider. Did this unicorn just make a saucy comment?

"Blaze, don't shock her even more," Storm admonishes him. Yes, it's definitely a him. His voice is melodically masculine, although I'm not quite sure how he manages to sound so human. Do horses have vocal chords? These are the moments

I miss the internet. It would be a quick search to find out, but here I have to either ask questions or not find out.

This time, I decide to stay quiet. I don't want to embarrass myself in front of this unicorn. Who knows how powerful he is. A bit of healthy respect won't hurt.

"We bring food," Frost says and shows the unicorn our basket. "Can we have our picnic at your place?"

"You want to bring a girl into my house? And probably be loud? And eat human food? Hell yes!"

His bright blue eyes shimmer in excitement. Looks like this unicorn isn't used to having visitors. Really his own fault, living under a tree isn't very inviting. Only the initiated would ever find his dwelling.

"No flirting," Storm warns as Blaze moves back towards his hole. How did he fit through there? The unicorn is decidedly too big for that.

"Yeah, yeah, I'll behave," Blaze mutters and dissolves into rainbow mist. He definitely has a flair for drama. But if you're a unicorn, you're allowed to be a little flashy.

Chapter Three

Storm takes the lead, stepping into the mist where the hole just was. I expect him to fall, but nothing happens. It looks as if he's still standing on solid ground. Weird. Magic is so weird.

"Watch and learn," he grins and stamps once with his right foot. Then he sinks into the earth.

It's like he's standing on an elevator that's slowly going down. He stands there patiently, watching my reaction as he descends ever further. When only his head is above ground, he winks. Storm is enjoying this, that much is clear. Am I going to see more of the playful Storm today? I very much hope so. He's been so serious recently, taking on his old role in the Palace. He deserves to have some fun. Preferably with me on a blanket. Without the unicorn.

"Want to go next?" Crispin asks me and I nod, not sure whether I should look forward to this. It doesn't seem as much fun as the slides in the Palace towers.

I step into the mist, almost afraid that the hole might have returned, but no, I stand on something hard. Harder than the ground, maybe wood or stone?

Just like Storm, I stamp my right foot – and nothing happens. I look at my Guardians questioningly.

"Maybe try harder?" Frost suggests. "Storm's a lot heavier than you."

I stamp again, this time with as much force as I can muster. It works. The ground vibrates, then I'm slowly transported down.

Darkness awaits me. It's a long shaft that takes me down further and further. Who has ever heard of unicorns living underground? Maybe he's eccentric even for a unicorn?

It takes several minutes and I'm getting bored. Yes, I definitely prefer the sliding stairs. I've tried them all in the past two weeks, discovering that they all have different speeds and curves. It's my favourite thing about living in my mother's Palace.

Finally, the platform I'm standing on comes to a halt. I step off it, looking around. It's dark everywhere with the exception of a dim light in the distance. Carefully, I walk towards it, a bit annoyed that Storm didn't wait for me. The ground is uneven and I'd really like some lamps. Or a Guardian, either works.

"Storm?" I call out.

"Over here!" he responds. He's close and I walk into the direction of his voice. It slowly grows a little brighter and my steps become more confident. It's as if the walls themselves are giving off a faint glow. Bioluminescence? Magic?

"Just around the corner!" he calls. Why is he hiding from me? Couldn't he just have waited? I grumble to myself as I step around the corner and –

Wow.

Imagine a rainbow trapped into a cave of mirrors, reflecting itself over and over again. Then add a sexy Guardian sitting on the ground with a picnic basket, holding up a bottle of something that looks like my favourite red wine. And to top it all off, there are strawberries in a bowl on the picnic blanket.

Wow. This is the pinnacle of romance. I just want to throw myself at him and... no. Let's wait for the others.

"Dragon got your tongue?" Storm asks and opens the bottle with a gentle pop.

"Where's Blaze?" I ask, looking around for the unicorn. If I start getting touchy-feely, I better make sure there are no witnesses.

"He's gone to get himself some food from the larder. As much as he pretends to love human food, he can't stomach it." He beckons me to sit down next to him.

"Are the others coming?" I ask him, finding it a bit strange that they're not here already.

"Yes, in a moment. I wanted to talk to you for a second, just the two of us."

I take a seat on the blanket opposite Storm, looking at him curiously. His words are really quite ominous... should I be scared? Is it going to be some kind of bad news?

"Okay... what's up?" I cross my legs and try to look comfortable despite the tension within me. People saying they want to talk is never a good sign.

"I'm sorry I haven't been around much lately," he begins and I nod. Yup, he's right about that. He's been absent a lot. "I talked to your mother about it."

"You did what?" I gape at him. Why would he talk to Beira about our private life?

"She's allowed me to reduce my working hours so I can spend more time with you. Same for the others. But I want to make some rules. We each get to spend some alone time with you. We can be all together in the evenings or for excursions like this one, but I want more of you. I need more of you."

His gaze grows heated as he looks me straight into my eyes. Wow. Did he just say he needs me?

"I've missed you too," I say softly, not quite sure how to respond. I'm not very experienced with this kind of relationship talk. Usually I'd try and laugh about it and then change the topic. But it's clear Storm is very serious.

"When you say you need alone time... are you still okay with me being with, you know, all of you?"

I'm a bit scared of his reply. If he says no, I'd have no idea what to do.

"Yes, I am," he says and I breathe a sigh of relief. "But I do feel jealous sometimes when I know that you're with the others while I have to work. I don't want to be the one you're with the least. I want to be the one you spend the most amount of time with."

He grins sheepishly.

"Wouldn't that be unfair towards the others?" I ask and return his smile.

"Yeah, probably. But I'm the leader, so who cares." With that, he gets up and walks around the picnic basket before kneeling down in front of me.

"We've not known each other for very long, but the bond makes it feel as if we have. I get... I don't know how to say it... strange when I'm not around you."

"Anxious?" I try but he shakes his head. I think of how I've felt recently. "Like something is missing from inside you?"

He looks at me strangely. "Yes. Exactly that. It's like I'm drawn towards you, no matter where I am. It's very strange, like I've got a compass inside me pointing towards you. It's very distracting."

"Tell me about it," I murmur. "I've got four of those compasses." Now that he's used that image, I realise how well it fits.

Whenever I've been alone, I've felt not quite right. And that's been often recently. We've all been busy...

"As cute as you two are, I'm getting hungry," Blaze suddenly interrupts us from behind. I blush. How much did he hear? I'm not quite sure if I like this flamboyant unicorn. He's a bit too much.

"Guys, you can come in now!" Storm shouts and the other three Guardians enter the rainbow cave a moment later. Now that everybody is in here, it's getting a little crammed. Blaze isn't exactly a small unicorn.

"Strawberries!" Crispin exclaims and pops one into his mouth immediately. I can already see that I need to be fast with eating them. Strawberries are my favourite. And discovering that they exist in the Realm is a welcome surprise. I wonder if they have greenhouses somewhere? Or do they import them from

Earth? There's so much I still need to learn about the workings of this place. So far, I've never even thought about where the food we're served in the Palace is coming from. But there are no fields to grow anything on; the perpetual snow prevents the people here from farming.

Arc sits down next to me and pulls me close until I lean against his shoulder. He's nice and warm, and despite his hard muscles he's really quite comfy.

"Do ye like this place?" he asks, grinning as some rainbow light reflects on the glass he's filling with wine.

"It's unusual," I say diplomatically. "It reminds me of my heart cave, where my magic lives."

"Aye, yer strange magic. Is she getting easier ta deal with?"

I shake my head, not wanting to lie to him. "Not really."

"I think we need some training lessons," he says with a smile and a wink. I'm not sure his lessons will be all about my magic. "But first, let's see what else is in the basket."

"Let me," Storm grins and uses his wind magic to float the contents of the basket onto the blanket. I admire his precise control. I would likely have destroyed all the food or crashed it against the crystal ceiling. Yup, training is in my future.

There are several bowls of food, including some of my favourite dishes. Potato salad, fried samosas, little cinnamon cakes with a thick layer of frosting, meatballs, ... I have no idea how all that food fit into the basket. Magic, most likely. And most of the bowls aren't even covered with a lid. Weird.

A meatball floats towards me. Storm smiles as I open my mouth to let it enter, but it's too large and it almost falls down. He laughs and so do the others. Storm is in a really good mood suddenly. I like seeing him like this. Maybe it's being in a rainbow cave, maybe it reminds him of our time on that rainbow... I get all hot and flushed just thinking of that moment when I was with all of them - except for Crispin.

I look at my blond Guardian. He's reserving the carrot salad for himself, hugging the bowl with a cheeky grin on his face. He likes healthy food for some reason. Yet another thing I don't understand about Crispin. He's a mystery, hiding behind his smiles and winks. I had hoped he'd open up a bit more now that we're out of danger, but no such luck. Storm's idea of me spending some alone time with all of the guys is likely good for that. I might get a bit closer to Crispin... or at least understand why he keeps pushing me away.

"Who wants sparklies?" Blaze asks and the guys groan in response.

"Sparklies?" I ask, turning around to the unicorn who's prancing around in excitement.

"Yes, sparklies! Don't tell me you haven't heard about Blaze's famous sparklies?"

"I'm afraid not," I say, not quite sure how famous these things actually are. Judging from my Guardians' expressions, Blaze is the only one thinking them to be.

"Touch my horn," the unicorn says and I stare at it in confusion, ignoring the hidden innuendo in his flirty voice.

"Why?"

"To feel the sparklies, of course!"

I look at Storm who nods at me with a grin.

"Just a little," he warns Blaze and the unicorn bows his head in response.

I reach out to touch the unicorn's horn - and the strangest feeling takes hold of me. It's like bliss, happiness and contentment went out together and produced a child that's now clinging to my chest. Maybe this is what taking drugs feels like? I moan as my head becomes fuzzy and my breasts tighten. Is this supposed to happen? I don't care, it's lovely. Why has nobody given me sparklies before? Why haven't I met a unicorn before? Why am I not living with it in this beautiful rainbow cave? I should move in. I should love the unicorn like I love my...

Oh.

"I think you gave her a little too much," Crispin's stern voice tears through my fog of happiness. "She looks stoned."

"Not stoned, just happy," I mumble and snuggle against him as he takes me into his arms. "You're comfy."

He laughs. "Glad to hear it."

"I think I love you. And sparklies. I love sparklies."

"What did you do to her?" Storm asks, his voice not as funny as I would like it to be. "Did you give her too much?"

"Smile!" I tell him but he ignores me.

"Blaze, undo whatever you did," he growls, looking at me strangely. I hold out a hand and touch his cheek.

"You're not as soft as Crispy."

The Guardian holding me groans. "Did you just call me soft?"

I giggle. "Yes, soft and comfy and pretty. Stormy is harder. He should smile more."

"Blaze!" Storm snaps, ignoring me. "Stop her."

"You're so boring," the unicorn sighs but then he whinnies and all the happiness drains out of me. The sparkles I saw floating all around me in the air disappear and so does the warm fuzzy feeling in my belly. Reality crashes into me.

Oh.

What did I just say?

What did he do to me?

That unicorn is going to die.

I sit up from my comfy position on Crispin's lap and look around at my Guardians. None of them are meeting my gaze. Are they embarrassed?

As I said, death to the unicorn.

"Blaze, what was all that?" I ask him, trying to remain calm and measured.

"Was it fun?" he asks excitedly. "There's more where that came from."

"Did you know it would affect me like that?"

He blushes (yes, unicorns can blush). "I thought as a goddess you'd need twice the normal dose. I may have been a little wrong about that."

I give him a piercing look, the one I've learned from my mother. "So normally, people don't act like I just did?"

They look at each other.

"No, this was quite an unusual reaction," Frost finally says. "Most people just feel a bit happier than they did before, not as out of it as you. And I'm not sure if I liked seeing you like that or not." Leaving me blushing, he turns to Blaze. "You definitely overstepped the mark. This is the heiress to the Winter Throne and you made her act like a drugged teenager. You'll be lucky if we don't tell her Majesty."

The unicorn pouts. "I thought you'd like it. Not my fault she isn't used to anything."

"Wait, you assumed I was used to taking drugs?" I ask incredulously. "What kind of person do you think I am?"

Blaze sighs. "Apparently not the kind I thought you were. But maybe we can forget about this whole incident now and have some food?"

"Don't think I will forget," Storm growls. "You owe us, Blaze."

"How about some ice cream?" The unicorn is trying to change the topic, but flinches when he sees Storm's piercing eyes. "Okay, okay, I'll leave you alone for a bit."

He disappears into a cloud of rainbow mist.

"Is he really gone or still listening in?" I ask cautiously. I'm beginning to think this unicorn is capable of anything naughty by now.

"He won't be able to listen in," Storm explains. "He may disappear into that sparkly stuff, but he has to reappear somewhere else pretty quickly after. So he's definitely not floating around in here."

I sigh in relief. "Are all unicorns like him?"

Crispin chuckles. "He's the only one we know, so can't give you an informed opinion on that. They are solitary creatures and it was only by chance that we got to know Blaze. I think we're the only Guardians he's taken into his home. I guess it's an honour, but then... he's quite a handful."

"Tell me about it," I say, shivering at the memory of me behaving like a stoner. I can't quite remember what I said but I'm pretty sure it wasn't what I'd want them to know.

"Anyway, shall we follow his advice and have some food?" Frost asks, already chomping on a chicken drum.

"Aye, good idea," Arc agrees and pulls the bowl with the fried dough balls closer to himself. Pretty sure I won't see them again. When Arc chooses food, it's his food and his alone. He doesn't take prisoners when it comes to eating. It's one of the many things I like about him. It's cute, if annoying at times. Luckily there's enough other stuff spread out on our picnic blanket. I won't miss those dough balls - although I use my air magic to float one out of the bowl and into my mouth to make a point.

"Well done," Storm grins. "That was excellent control."

Wow. Yes, it was. It was so instinctive that I didn't even notice how little effort it took. My magic is so strange. One day she does exactly what I want her to, others she resists me with all her might. Or turns my intent into something a lot more destructive. Like the time I wanted to thaw the pond in one of the Palace's courtyards. I ended up having to call the healer for the burns some of the onlookers suffered. Not doing that again...

"Maybe I won't need those lessons after all," I boast, ferrying another dough ball over to me using my magic. Before it can reach my mouth, Crispin snatches it out of the air.

"I think you need some protect-your-dough-ball lessons," he chuckles as he bites into his stolen food. I elbow him gently - it's not as if I'm actually that keen on the balls. There are strawberries, after all.

Still, he whines as I hit him. Frost laughs loudly. "You need protect-your-own-balls lessons."

Crispin snorts. "My balls are well protected, thank you very much. Wyn is the only danger to them. Isn't that right, Princess?"

"Only if you're annoying," I tell him and bite into a juicy strawberry. Arc winces.

"Yer scary like that."

I look at him in confusion. "Scary? Me?"

"Ye talk aboot his balls and then bite into something just as soft." He shakes his head. "Nae good."

I laugh. "Are we really comparing Crispin's balls to strawberries? Is this the unicorn's influence?"

"Nope, just us being us," Frost says with a chuckle. "I've missed our banter. There's always been annoying things like work or demons. We need more time together."

"I couldn't agree more." I nod while trying to hide the strawberry juice that just dripped onto my clothes. Luckily there's a good magical washing basket at the Palace. You throw your clothes in and they come out perfectly washed and ironed. They even managed to wash out the blood stains I've acquired during the few training sessions I've had.

I wish I'd known that cleaning clothes spell when I lived back on Earth with my parents. That would have made my chores so much less annoying. I wonder what they're doing now. Are they missing me? Are they angry at me for destroying their home? Will they forgive me? What if they don't want to see me again? What if I'll never get the chance to apologise? I clear my throat as I feel myself choking up.

"Why are you looking so sad suddenly?" Storm asks, a touch of concern in his eyes.

"Thinking of my parents," I mumble, a bit embarrassed for suddenly turning emotional.

"I'm sure they're okay," Crispin says and gently strokes my back. His hands are warm and I lean into his touch. I could do with a hug right now.

"Beira said there was no easy way to contact them. It's too dangerous to send someone to them at the moment, not after the demons at Calanais. There may be some who've returned there, she said, and she can't risk any of her Guardians being hurt. But I need to know if they're alright." The last sentence turns into a whisper. I sound weak and I hate that I do. Now more than ever, I need to portray myself as a Princess, not an emotional young woman.

"I may ken a way," Arc says quietly. "It's not strictly speaking legal, though."

"What is it?" Storm asks, his brow furrowed at the thought of going against the law. He's one of the Queen's highest-ranking Guardians, so he's probably supposed to follow the rules.

"Sure ye want ta ken?"

"Maybe not. Tell Wyn and then she can decide whether to tell me and the others." Storm grins. "Plausible deniability."

"You know that my mother is the law and I kind of have to follow it as well?" I remember how my mother had to follow her own rules and send me away to Earth when I was born. There are some laws you have to abide by, even as the Queen. Or her heiress.

"It's nae that bad, lassie," Arc chuckles. "Shall I whisper it to ya?"

I nod and leave the warmth of Crispin's lap to climb over to Arc. He hugs me around the waist and pulls me close until his breath is hot on my ear.

Then he whispers his secret and my eyes widen. This is going to be naughty.

But waiting a week will be agony. Unless I find some distraction.

Chapter Four

I don't know why young girls want to be princesses. It's really quite boring. And uncomfortable. At least the dresses they make me wear are. No amount of magic can persuade my waist to fit into the corset one of the maids is trying to force on me. My body isn't made for this kind of feminine clothing. I want something loose, comfy, not these torturous, squeezing, unflattering dresses. Unfortunately, I'm the only one of that opinion. My mother with her Goddess genes wears whatever she wants in the most effortless way, one day sporting a tiny waist and the next curves in all the right places. It's as if she can change her appearance at will.

I can't. I'm stuck with my bony hips and my boobs that aren't small enough for the corset but small enough to look strange in some of the deep neckline dresses. I'm tempted to ask my mother for trousers and hoodies. All I've achieved so far is getting to choose the colours in my wardrobe. Baby steps, even though I'm the Princess.

When I walk around the Palace, people keep following me, waiting for instructions. Or to hear the latest gossip. Or to tell me the latest gossip. Basically, they want attention and think that I can give it to them. I'm becoming an expert at noncommittal nods, polite smiles and gentle handwaving. They've even brought children to me to be blessed. I had no clue what to do when that baby was shoved into my arms. I have no idea about kids, and even less about how to bless someone. Surely my mother is the Goddess with the powers of creation, not me? I'm just her offspring, half Guardian, half Goddess. All I have is some magic, but nothing like the powers my mother has.

Then there are the people looking for my opinion. I'm not a member of my mother's Council, and I prefer it that way. It will take me some time to get used to the politics of this place, unfamiliar as they are. But there are some of her courtiers who seem to think that they better start early. They flatter me, they send me presents, they pretend they're more important than they actually are. Most of the time, I see through them. Sometimes, I need to ask my Guardians or Tamara to find out what those people want from me. And if even my friends don't know, then they're probably not worth my time. Otherwise I'd spend all my days entertaining nobles and listening to gossip. As much fun as the latter can be, I have better things to do. Like spending time with my Guardians.

Storm is taking me out tonight. It's the first time we'll be alone since we arrived in the Realm. I think it's a date - I hope it is. But when I think back to the heat in his eyes in the unicorn cave, I'd be surprised if this was just a chat amongst friends.

"You need to draw in your belly and hold your breath while I do this, your Highness," the chambermaid sighs as I repel the corset once again. It's not compatible with my body.

"I think Storm will have to take me without a corset," I

proclaim to her shocked gasp. "He's seen me without one before. It's not like lots of people wear them on Earth."

"But Mistress, it's the fashion here..."

"Am I the Princess?" I ask and she goes very quiet. I hate to be like that, but right now, it's necessary.

"Yes, I'm sorry, your Highness. Forgive me."

"It's forgiven. Now run along, I'm going to choose something else to wear. I don't need your help for that."

She hurries away, shooting me some very disappointed glances. She was probably hoping to be praised by the Heiress of the Winter Throne, maybe even chosen as my personal maid. Most of the girls doing this job are the same. But I don't want a maid, I don't want any of the servants. I'm used to dealing with my wardrobe on my own. And I hate corsets. What's so hard to understand about that?

I sigh as I look into my closet. There's not much usable stuff in there. I've decided not to wear a dress. I want to look like when Storm first got to know me: human. Or maybe not human, but normal. Not a princess. Just me, Wyn, the woman from Edinburgh who has trouble with her magic and is in love with four men instead of one. Why can't the others here just accept that? I'm not one of them, not like my mother. I didn't grow up here, so I shouldn't be expected to fit in like this.

There's only one way to get out of this. Tamara.

I ring the bell next to the marble doorframe. It's not connected to anything, but somehow Tamara will be notified. Magic. As always.

A moment later, she knocks on the door, but before I can call for her to enter, she sweeps into the room, a wide smile on her face.

"How can I help, my lady?"

"Stop the ladying. I need jeans. And a normal shirt. And shoes without heels. Human clothes with no frills and unnecessary fabric. I need a break from all those dresses."

She gives me a knowing smile. "As you wish. Your mother won't be pleased though. Neither will the maids. They've planned out your wardrobe for the next few months and have drawn lots for who gets to dress you."

I shudder. "Torture," I murmur. "I didn't think torture would await me here. But somehow these girls manage to slowly kill me with every dress."

"Come on, it's not that bad," Tamara laughs. "And you can't tell me you haven't seen the looks your men give you when you wear one of those dresses. Especially the dark blue see-through one."

Oh yes, I remember that. The only place where the fabric wasn't semi-translucent was a patch above my boobs and one around my waist. No wonder my guys liked it. Although they would have liked it even more if I'd taken it off - but of course they had to work, so I was left alone in my pretty dress.

Princessing sucks sometimes.

I find Storm in one of the courtyards. He's not wearing a shirt and his wings are exposed, glittering in the afternoon sun. They're as wide as he is tall and just as strong. Here in the

Realms, it's obvious how different the Guardians are from humans. They're more like angels. Even now as he moves from one battle stance to another, he's got something angelic about him.

With every step, his muscles ripple. My fingers twitch as I imagine running my hands over his back, his chest...

"Stop staring!" he suddenly calls without looking at me. Does he have eyes in the back of his head?

Embarrassed, I step out of the shadows and approach my Guardian. The man who had to learn to smile, but who's a lot more relaxed now that we no longer face demons on a daily basis. He even jokes from time to time, still surprising me with every pun. He's got a good sense of humour, even if he doesn't often show it. He probably thinks he has to keep up his leader persona. And to be honest, I quite like his dominant side.

"If you don't want me to stare, you should put on a shirt," I tell him and he turns around, showing me his glistening upper body. He must have been working out for a while.

"Now why would I do that?" he asks and slowly stalks towards me. "I like that look in your eyes."

"A moment ago you told me not to stare."

"Oh. That was a mistake. Stare as much as you like."

He presents his beautiful sapphire wings and shakes them before folding them up behind his back. I know that if I was to walk around him, they'd disappeared. It still boggles my mind how our wings are there and not at the same time. Where do they go when we don't use them? Especially his, they don't look as translucent and light as mine.

Storm waves his hands and a breeze starts to blow around him, drying his skin within seconds. A black shirt that was lying on the ground floats up and he puts it on, covering the splendid view.

"No more staring?" I ask in disappointment.

"Later," he promises with a wink. "First, let's have our date."

"Are we going to fly somewhere?"

"In a way…" He smirks and butterflies tremble in my belly. He's going to get me all weak and needy with that look in his eyes. The one that promises fire and passion.

He suddenly hugs me and I melt into his embrace.

"Hold on tight!" he whispers before a roaring wind surrounds us. Storm's body temperature is warming me despite the two layers of fabric between us. Maybe we can get rid of them later.

The wind gets stronger until we're lifted off the ground. My hair is blown all around my head and I press my face to Storm's chest so none of the strands get into my eyes. Despite the noise of the storm, it actually feels quite cosy, being snuggled against my Guardian. He makes me feel safe even in moments where I feel safe already. Don't ask me how that works, but I like it.

We're getting faster as we fly upwards. I shiver in the cold wind but a moment later the air around me gets warm. Storm must have noticed. How considerate.

We land gently on a smooth surface. I open my eyes, only now noticing that I had them closed for the entire flight. Not that I was scared, but it was cosier that way. I trusted him not to drop me.

I untangle myself from Storm's embrace and look around. We're on a tower at the edge of the Palace, but this one is different from all the rest. It's made from a glistening white material, marble maybe? It's got thin veins of silver running through the stone, making it shimmer even more in the pale sunlight this Realm is known for.

There doesn't seem to be an exit from this tower. No stairs, not even a trapdoor. Just a smooth, large platform surrounded by marble railings. No wonder we had to fly up here. But who builds a tower you can't actually exit from below? That's just weird.

The space we're standing on is about half the size of the Palace's Great Hall, which means it's massive. In the centre, a table and two chairs are waiting for us. Is Storm really doing a proper date with me? With food and a view and romance?

Wow. I need to pinch myself. This is so unlike him. Did he get one of the other Guardians to help him plan this? Or maybe Tamara? I can imagine her giving him pointers at how to create a proper date. Looks like he listened.

I walk towards the table and Storm follows me. It's only now that I notice the white rose petals on the ground. Really? It's almost getting a bit over the top now. I've never been on a date like this. Guys usually took me to a cafe or bar for a drink, if they were interested. Getting some salty pretzels was the epitome of a good date on Earth. But this is... special.

Beautiful.

Amazing.

On the table is a bottle and two champagne flutes, together with a bowl of strawberries.

I turn and look at Storm in wonder.

"Strawberries?"

He smiles. "It's hard not to notice how much you love them."

He steps behind one of the iron wrought chairs and pulls it back a little, gesturing me to sit down. Wow, Storm the gentleman. It's as if he's done it thousands of times. That makes me think. Maybe he has? How many dates has he been on? How many girls have there been?

Stop it, Wyn. Don't ruin this with those kind of thoughts. He's lived for a long time, of course there have been others. Just because I'm only twenty-two doesn't mean my Guardians are.

"Would you like some wine?" he asks and fills my glass when I nod. He sits down opposite me and takes his own glass in one hand.

"To a lovely evening," he says and we clink glasses. The wine is slightly sweet but not enough to give me a headache tomorrow. Yes, even Demigoddesses get hangovers.

Then we sit in silence. Am I supposed to say something? What do we talk about? The Summer King threat? The demons we slew? My choice of dress?

To hide my moment of insecurity, I take a strawberry. It's juicy and sweet and perfect.

"Did you know your eyes light up when you eat them?" Storm asks with a grin.

I swallow before answering - yes, the whole Princess etiquette training has paid off. "Do they? Does that mean I get to eat more of them?"

He shrugs. "There's a whole bowl just for you. I'm not that big a fan."

I stare at him in shock. "You don't like strawberries?!"

"It's not that I dislike them. I just don't care much about them. There are better fruit. Like blueberries, freshly picked after a bout of snow. Or apples drenched in honey. Or... sorry, we're not really here to talk about food."

"Then what are we here to talk about?" I blurt before I can stop myself.

He looks at me strangely. "Us? And the others, I guess. But I'm not sure how much talking I was planning to do."

Gods save my hormones. Is he really suggesting what I think he is?

"Shall we have some food first?" he asks and destroys my thoughts of my Guardian's lips on mine. But then my stomach growls softly and I decide I need some proper food. Then I can feast on Storm.

"That would be lovely," I say, popping another strawberry into my mouth. Who knows if he'll leave them there when he adds more items to the table, so I better plan ahead. I take another few and put them on my napkin.

I look up and see Storm grinning at me.

"I wasn't going to take them away from you."

I huff. "Well, you never know. You may have held them hostage in return for favours."

"Does that mean you're not going to give those... favours willingly later on?"

I smirk. "That depends on what exactly you want."

He winks and my insides melt a little at his suggestive look. "You'll find out soon. But first, food."

He closes his eyes for a moment and a second later, several bowls appear on the table. It's not built for this much and some of the plates are precariously close to the edge. I hope my clumsiness won't turn this into a massive accident full of shards and spilt food. But as long as I stay on my chair, it should be fine.

Storm opens one of the bowls and a cloud of steam escapes, revealing six perfectly formed dumplings covered in powdery sugar. From past experience and a long chat with the cook, I know that they're filled with poppy seed and plum jam. Best combination ever. Now we just need... Yes! My Guardian hands me a carafe filled with vanilla custard. Perfect.

At this point I should say that yes, I love sugary food. And I can eat it at any time of day. If it was up to me, savoury food wouldn't have to exist. At all. Give me strawberries and dumplings any day.

Storm doesn't seem to agree. He's filled his plate with a steak, mashed potatoes and a giant puddle of gravy. No vegetables though.

"You should be eating some vitamins," I tell him sternly while nibbling on a strawberry. "See, I'm getting mine. You want to stay a healthy and strong Guardian."

He chuckles. "Don't worry, I'll get my exercise soon."

I look at him wide-eyed. "What's happened to you? Did you have a run in with an incubus?" I think for a moment, trying to remember whether I read about incubi in my mother's factual library or in a novel back home on Earth. "Do they exist?"

Storm laughs even more now. "No, they don't. And I'm just a bit more relaxed than usual. And I got good news that I was waiting to tell you. I had planned to first have dinner, but why not now... Or maybe later."

He stops and I look at him sternly. "Tell me. Now."

"Your mother has given me a week off. I'll be able to spend a lot more time with you."

A smile makes its way from my heart to my lips. More time. With Storm. No more stolen kisses while we meet in a corridor. Actual time where we can talk and have fun and do other things.

"Just you or the others as well?" I ask and my smile dims as I see his expression dim. Stupid Wyn, don't remind him that there are others. Let's just have a proper date, just the two of us. But I can't just shove my other three Guardians from my mind and my heart. They're all entwined, and not just because of the bond we formed.

I never thought I could love several people equally. My mother told me that it was possible, although she was talking about loving your children and partner just as much. Just in different ways. And it's the same with my men, I love them all in their own, special way.

"All of us," Storm replies gruffly. "But we've agreed we'll each get to spend a day with you. That still leaves three days for all five of us to be together."

"Sounds good." I make an extra effort to brighten my smile so he sees how much I value my time with him. I want him to feel special. He's my Storm, after all. My beautiful, harsh, dark Storm. I remember how I first met him and chuckle.

"What's the matter?" he asks and I grin.

"Just remembering what I thought when I first saw you."

He frowns. "Wow, what a good-looking Guardian?"

"No, more like 'who is that brooding man in a cloak'. I'm glad you're no longer wearing that thing, it made you look like a Nazgul."

"A what?"

"A ringwraith? Black rider? Have you never read Lord of the Rings?"

He looks at me in confusion. "Is that a human book?"

I nod.

"Then of course I haven't. And by the way, cloaks are very fashionable."

I smirk. "I've not seen anyone here wear one like yours. The guards' cloaks are a lot less... gloomy."

"I prefer mysterious. Dark and mysterious and alluring." He draws a hand through his hair and tries to give me a seductive wink. He fails. I laugh and he growls.

"Don't laugh at my mysteriousness."

"I wouldn't dare to."

Finally, he no longer manages to stay serious and a smile brightens his face. He's so pretty when he smiles, but of course I won't tell him that. His ego is big enough as it is.

To distract myself from the draw I feel towards him, I eat another strawberry. Only when I take a second do I notice that he's still watching me.

"Something the matter?"

"I just noticed that I'm… happy."

I shrug. "And how is that special?"

He clears his throat. "I've not felt this way in a long time. Before I was sent to get you, my life was nothing but work. Maybe drinking at night with my friends, but I never had the time to feel like this. Like the sun has broken through a thick layer of clouds and is now warming me with its rays."

"Wow, aren't you a poet," I tease him, but inside, I'm touched. I'm pretty sure Storm doesn't usually share his feelings like that. "So if I'm the sun, does that mean I get to warm you?"

Oops, that last sentence wasn't supposed to come out that way. I blame the hormones that are sizzling through my lower body whenever I look at him. Especially when his gaze is fixed on me like now.

Instead of a response, the table between us lifts into the air - I just about manage to snatch one final strawberry - and floats to one side, leaving nothing between me and my Guardian. A moment later, my chair begins to shake and I'm thrown towards Storm who catches me out of the air.

"That's cheating," I whisper as he sits me on his lap until I face him.

"What am I cheating at?" he asks, his voice a tiny bit hoarse. Oh Gods is he hot. Not warm hot, sexy hot.

"Being not attractive."

"I didn't know I was trying to be that." He chuckles slightly and his chest vibrates against mine. "Now what are we going to do now?"

I smile evilly. "We could talk about politics."

"I'm sure we could. How about we do something a little more fun?"

He runs his hands over my back and I'm glad I'm wearing a normal shirt and not one of those frilly dresses with too many layers of fabric. I want to feel his touch, his warmth. I wrap my legs around his hips and put my hands on his shoulders, pulling myself even closer to him. I lower my lips to his and am amazed at how soft they feel. Just like every time. I can't connect this softness with his otherwise hard, unyielding body. And mind. He's one of the strongest people I know. But there are parts of him that are gentle and soft, and I'm not talking about his body. Although his lips… I kiss him, first slowly, savouring every second, then more urgently until I'm gasping for air. He returns the kiss, demanding access to my mouth, his tongue dancing around mine, fighting a romantic duel.

His hands slip under my shirt and pull it up. He's impatient, just like me. There won't be a long foreplay today. Suits me. It's been too long.

I moan as he pulls back so he can lift the shirt over my arms and head. Just those few seconds without his lips on mine are torturous. I need him, more of him. Everything of him, every atom needs to be with me. In me.

Then his mouth is back on mine, his lips sucking on mine, while he fumbles with the catch of my bra. I'm debating whether to help him but I'm busy kissing. My brain can't focus on anything else just now. All there is are my swollen lips against his. And luckily, he manages by himself, and with a click the bra opens.

I grate my hips against his pelvis and his hardness. He's ready, and through the wetness of my panties I can feel how ready I am myself. That must have been one of the quickest dates ever. At least I got to eat a few strawberries. And now I'm eating Storm.

He slides my bra down my arms, exposing my breasts into the cool evening air. My nipples are hard, waiting for his touch. He takes one between two fingers and gently rolls it between them. Little lightning bolts run straight from my breasts down to the ache between my legs. I'm hungry, so hungry.

I suck on his bottom lip, then bite a little. He groans as my teeth scrape against his lip, but he doesn't protest. On the contrary, he stops moving his head to give me more access. I nibble a bit more, not daring to draw blood.

Storm cups my arse and lifts me up to change my position slightly. I'm now sitting even closer to him, even more on his hardness. But with me sitting on his lap, I can't even reach his jeans to release him. So all I can do is grind my hips, rubbing myself against him. This is not enough. Did I think that before? Am I really so insatiable?

I guess I am.

He plays with my nipples again, both, this time. I moan and by accident, I bite down a little too hard on his lip. The metallic taste of blood fills my mouth. Oops.

I stop, thinking that Storm is going to be angry. But he groans again and whispers hoarsely, "Do it again."

I smile. So he likes the biting. Well, I can deal with that.

While I press my teeth into his lip, he squeezes my nipples harder, almost to the point where it hurts. It feels good.

So good.

"More!" I moan and he continues to play with them,

squeezing and pulling them until my skin is stretched to the max.

It's never been this rough between us. I mean, I know it can get a lot rougher, I'm not that innocent, but this is new. But it fits.

I leave his mouth and draw my lips along his cheek until I reach his neck. Like a vampire, I latch onto his skin and bite. I wouldn't be surprised if I suddenly grew fangs, but alas, that is not a skill Demigoddesses seem to possess.

I don't draw blood but I love the feeling of my mouth on his skin, my teeth pressing against his flesh. Leaving one hand on my left breast, squeezing it tightly, he opens my trousers with his other, managing to pull down the zip. He slips inside and almost immediately, one finger enters my core. I moan loudly as he moves it in me, exploring my innermost sanctum.

I forget all about biting him, instead I hold onto his shoulders and arch my back to give him better access.

Without warning, I'm lifted into the air until I'm hovering just above him. Magic while having sex? Who would say no to that?

With me in the air, Storm gets up and pulls down his jeans, exposing his hard erection. He takes off his shirt as well and I almost begin to drool. How do I deserve someone as gorgeous as him?

When he's naked, he looks at me as I float in front of him. My breasts are exposed, my trousers open but still mostly in position.

"Don't move," he says and steps forward, gently touching my cheek with two fingers. "You're beautiful."

He walks around me, his fingers trailing a line on my skin. When he reaches my feet, he slips off my shoes and begins to pull down my trousers. I'm still wearing my panties, wet with my own juices. He leaves them on and steps back again, inspecting me from a distance. I move my arms as if I'm swimming, hoping to move towards him. I want his touch, I need it.

"Don't," he whispers. "Stay, I like seeing you like that."

I moan in frustration but stop trying to move. The air is holding me in place, and even though I'm hovering several feet above the ground, I trust Storm completely. I'm safe with him, he won't let me fall.

He continues to walk around me, inspecting me from every angle. What is he doing? I have to admit though that it feels really quite erotic, being looked at like that. His eyes are hungry and it's obvious that he's having to hold himself back from ravishing me. At least that's what I'd like to think that expression on his face means. The dilated pupils, the furrowed brow, the small gap between his lips. Perfection.

"Touch yourself," he says, quietly but firmly. Oh, is he going to be all dominant now?

I'd rather he come over here and plunge into my depths... but I'm sure that's going to come at some point. I slip a hand under the rim of my panties and begin to draw small circles over my bud. I'm wet and ready for a lot more than just my fingers. I slide one finger into myself, then add another while my thumb still continues to rub. I moan as I'm starting to find my rhythm. If I wanted, I could come any moment now. But no. I'm going to wait for Storm.

Surprisingly, the air supports me as I arch my back and spread my thighs further. Storm walks a few steps until he stands at my feet with a perfect view of what I'm doing.

"Please," I whisper, hoping that he'll know what I mean.

"Not yet."

"I'm so close, I need you!" My whisper turns into a whimper as I slow down my pace to prevent myself from climaxing too soon. That bastard, torturing me like that.

"You'll manage," he chuckles and I moan as I see him touching himself. He strokes his length while watching me push two fingers into my depths. He's hard and erect. Beautiful. He was created as a perfect man, and here I am, with him, separated by nothing but air. Of course I could use my magic to get closer to him, to break the spell he's put over me, but that's not what I want. I'll wait for his permission.

"Add another finger. Prepare yourself for me," he instructs and I do as he says. I'm wet enough that it's not too much of a stretch at first, but when I start to move my hand back and forth, I do feel how tight I still am. But Storm has fit before and he will again.

Hungrily he watches me and I capture his gaze, willing him to come to me.

And then he does.

With two strides he's between my legs and I push my panties to one side just in time for him to enter me. Waves of pleasure run through me as he begins to move, setting a fast rhythm from the start. This isn't soft and romantic, this is a claiming, passionate and firm. He grips my hips and pulls me close with every thrust, slamming into me harder and harder.

Tingles begin to spread through my body and I can no longer hold back the moans. Every time he moves in me, I feel our connection grow, as if a part of him is entering me, not just with our bodies, but with our minds.

We ride together to ecstasy, when my wings unfold and wrap around us.

We're one.

Chapter Five

I wake up and something is wrong. There was a noise that woke me. Was there?

I'm in my bedroom, wrapped in one of the Palace's amazing blankets that are both light as silk and warm as wool.

Why am I in my bedroom?

Oh yes. Last night. Storm. Lots of Storm.

Where is he? Why is my head feeling so heavy? Did I drink too much? Did we drink?

Strawberries. Yes, I remember those. But would they make my head feel like this?

There's a strange taste in my mouth. Bitter.

My stomach lurches and I turn to one side, trying to stop the heaving. But too late, I empty the contents of my stomach onto the mattress. My puke is red. That can't be a good sign.

Weakly, I try to sit up and call for help. I'm ill and I want someone here with me.

There's a noise again, coming from the corner furthest away from me. A shadow… no, a man. Or a woman, it's hard to tell. The shape is kind of blurred. I blink, but it stays strangely blurry, just like the rest of the room. Do I suddenly need glasses? What's going on?

"Who are you?" I whisper, the bile in my throat making my voice almost inaudible.

"I'm Death," the person says in a rattling voice that makes me shiver. It's neither male nor female, just flat and cold. I'm beginning to shake as the dark shape comes closer. There's something in their hand, a vial?

"I am *your* Death."

Darkness is taking over my vision and I fight to stay conscious. There's pain in my head and my body and my skin is starting to itch.

I want to use my magic to get rid of this *Death*, whoever they are, but I'm too weak, I can't even access my heart cave. In a last attempt to do something, anything, before the person reaches me, I tug on the bond that connects me to my Guardians, hoping that it'll be strong enough for them to notice.

Then I can fight no longer and darkness claims me.

I'm on the floor when I wake up. It's cold and uncomfortable. I was in my bed before, right? Where is my bed? Where am I?

I scramble to my feet and look around. I'm in a circular room with a low ceiling that makes me feel slightly claustrophobic.

If I was to stand on my toes, I could easily touch it. The walls are made of doors, dozens of them. There's nothing between them, it's one door next to another. They're all made of the same dull metal that's rather uninviting. They make me think of prison doors.

"Hello?" I call out, but of course nobody answers. I'm alone here. I walk closer along the wall of doors, trying to see if there are any signs or hints to show where they may lead. Nothing. I don't even detect a scratch on the metal. They're flawless and boring.

I do a quick count. Sixteen doors. The room is a hexadecagon (my maths teacher would be proud), but I have no idea if that is relevant.

Sitting here wondering won't bring me any further. Maybe my magic can help me out? I reach into myself, searching for my heart cave where my magic resides.

I run into a barrier. There's something blocking me from reaching the cave. A solid, hard, threatening barrier built around it. I fly through my body, looking for another access. Nothing. I'm blocked from using my magic.

The realisation that I'm without her once more slams into me. Not again. I feel only half like myself without her. Like part of my soul is missing.

Who's done this to me? Come here so I can kill you. Without my magic. So maybe not kill. More like scratch.

So I don't have magic and I don't have a clue what I'm doing here. I can either sit here and wait or choose a random door and explore. And, as I've never been someone who likes to stay in one place and be bored, I walk straight ahead and open the first door I reach.

It leads into a brightly lit corridor. The walls and floor are made from the same dull metal as the door, while the ceiling is made of light. Not an electric light, but just... light. It's cold and unfriendly.

I hurry through the corridor, waiting for it to end. There's nothing that indicates where it leads. This could be anywhere, except that I have an inkling that it's magical. So probably not Earth.

At the end of the corridor, there's another door, just like the ones before. This time, I knock. I don't know why, it just feels right.

No answer. I press down the handle and push, but nothing happens. It's locked.

"You need to pull!" someone calls from inside. Embarrassed, I pull and the door opens. Every. Single. Time. At least there's no push/pull sign here, that would be even more embarrassing. My parents always made fun of me that I ignored those signs and then struggled with opening doors. Guess that hasn't changed.

I enter a small room that looks like the most stereotypical office you can imagine. Lot of shelves on the walls, overflowing with folders and books. A large desk with stacks of papers, and behind it, an elderly man. He looks human except for his slightly glowing eyes. They remind me of a cat at night. His skin is thin and papery, while his hair is almost gone and the remaining strands are a pale white. He looks like he's been in this office without sunlight for far too long.

He takes a form from one of the stacks and dips an old-fashioned pen into an inkwell.

"Name?" he asks in a drawling voice.

"What?"

"Name."

"Wyn. Ehm, Wynter."

"Surname."

"Ehm..." Since moving to my mother's Realm, I've not used my adoptive parents' name anymore. In the Palace, everybody calls me Princess or Your Highness, so I've not needed to think about what name to use. It feels strange using that Earth name. It's no longer me, I've changed. I should choose something new, something that fits the person I've become.

Something Royal.

"Prince. Wynter Prince."

"Why are you here, Wynter Prince?"

"You tell me?"

He looks up from the form he's filling in.

"Please answer my questions. Why are you here?"

I sigh. "I don't know. I was sleeping, then there was someone who called himself Death, and now I'm here. I didn't come here voluntarily, so I'd like to leave, please."

The man's expression doesn't change. "There is no person called Death."

"Yes, I assumed that," I say in exasperation. "But that's what he... she... they called themselves."

"Let's ignore that question..." He draws a long dash over part of the form.

"Next one: Where are you from?"

"Earth," I say automatically, then hesitate. "Although I was born in the Winter Realm and am now living there again."

"Oh, you're one of Beira's?" He's suddenly a little more interested.

"Yes, I'm her daughter."

Now I've got his full attention. "Oh, you're that Wynter. I've got your entry somewhere, give me a moment."

He gets up and begins to search through one of the largest bookshelves behind him. It holds dozens, if not hundreds of old tombs and volumes, most of them covered in a layer of dust. He runs a finger along their spines, rapidly reading their titles.

On the top shelf, he finally finds what he's been looking for. He pulls down a book that could have easily been split into several. It's thicker than any I've ever seen.

He opens it and goes through the index.

"Demi-gods of the Realms... yes... Memnon... No... Achilles... No... Tityos... No.... Wynter, Daughter of Beira. There you are. Page 1478."

He flicks through the pages, ignoring the dust that ascends into the air whenever he turns a page.

"1476... 1478. Wynter."

He begins to read and I'm tempted to walk around the desk to see what he's reading. I'm in a book? A very old one at that? A book about Demi-gods? There must be a lot of knowledge in there that could help me. I still don't know the full extent of my powers. Maybe it's all in there, maybe even instructions on how I can fulfil my potential. Preferably without hurting anyone. That's the reason I couldn't grow up with my mother in her Realm. Demi-gods have killed people before when they came into their powers - accidents, mostly, but not something my mother could chance.

"Very interesting," the man mumbles, but he doesn't seem interested in telling me what he's reading. "Oh yes, that makes sense..."

"Excuse me. Could you tell me what it says in there about me?"

"Huh?"

"I'd like to know what you're reading. If it's about me, I've got a right to know."

He looks confused.

"Yes, I guess so. But you'll have to fill in form 938B for that. Nobody is allowed to borrow a book without first filling in that form. I assume you have a library card?"

I stare at him in confusion. "I don't suppose you'd accept my Edinburgh Libraries card?"

"Any library card is fine. It's about the principle, you understand?"

I nod noncommittally. I have no clue what he's on about.

He hands me a yellow form and a pen. There's no space to write on his overfull desk, so I use the chair in front of me as a substitute.

Form 938B: Book Loan Contract.

There's a long list of terms and conditions at the beginning and I only skim them. Paragraph 48 catches my eye though: *Non-return of a book may result in decapitation.*

Wow, that's pretty harsh. Being killed for not returning a book to a library?

I read the remaining points a little more carefully, just in case, but none are as extreme as paragraph 48.

At the bottom of the form I fill in the book's title, my name - using Wynter Prince - and do a quick signature.

"Here you go." I hand him the form, but he only puts it on one of his overflowing in-trays.

"I'll look at it later. Now shush."

"But what am I supposed to do now? How do I get back home?"

He sighs. "Patience. First, I have to register you. Then we need to do some tests. Then you can fill in a release form and then we have to wait for an appropriate transport."

"Listen, I'm the Heiress to the Winter Throne, daughter of the Mother of Gods. I demand that you bring me home this instant!"

I put all the authority I can muster into my voice, but he doesn't even twitch an eyebrow.

"Child, here in the Library of Lives, everybody's equal. We all have to fill in the forms or there'd be chaos. Now sit down and let me work."

I ignore his request. "The Library of Lives? What's that?"

He looks up at me, his brow furrowed in confusion. "How can you not know where you are? People only get here if they request access... or if they're dead. And as you're not translucent, I assume... unless... oh."

"What?"

"Is this your first death experience?"

I laugh hysterically. "I'm not dead. And I've never died before, if that's what you mean."

"Ah, that explains a lot." He smiles and rummages through one of his desk drawers until he finds a small leaflet. He hands it to me.

"Read that, it'll explain things."

A Guide to Immortality.

There's a picture of a friendly old woman on the front, but not much else. I open the brochure and begin to read.

Dear Deceased,

It may come as a shock to you that you have died. Don't worry, this is not the end. Please try not to panic while you read this short Guide to Immortality.

If you've been given this leaflet, your advisor assumes that you are eligible for Immortality. This may be because of your heritage, your achievements or your good karma.

Being eligible for Immortality does not make you Immortal per se. You will need the right mindset to be able to apply and be chosen for Immortality. If you are unsure whether you have what it takes, please speak to your advisor.

> *Benefits of Immortality:*
>
> *- Indefinite existence*
>
> *- Immunity to all diseases*
>
> *- Endless relationships with other Immortals*
>
> *- Experience millennia of history, evolution and advances*

- The power to achieve genuine good

- Making a lot of money.

Disadvantages of Immortality:

- Outliving relatives and friends = centuries of loneliness and grief

- Boredom

- You may experience the world's end

- Insanity is a possibility.

Please be aware that, while you won't be able to die from disease, there are ways to kill an Immortal (decapitation, immolation and in extreme cases, starvation). We cannot be held responsible for your life ending earlier than planned even if you have chosen Immortality. For legal advice, please visit your Realm's Death Lawyer.

I look up from the leaflet in bewilderment. Surely this is a parody? An elaborate joke someone has set up? Immortality is not something you choose. It's something you have from birth, like Guardians or Gods. In my case, I was never quite sure. Some legends say Demi-gods are immortal, others say they aren't. What I am sure about is that I'll have a longer than average life. Unless I get killed.

"How do I... ehm... apply for Immortality?" I ask the old man and he clears his throat.

"There's a form somewhere... oh yes, here it is. You'll have to fill it in, then return it to me and I'll tell you what to do next."

"Can't you just tell me now?"

"No. It's procedure."

I sigh. This guy looks like he's been doing this job for hundreds of years. Bureaucracy must be all he can remember by now.

I look at the form he's handed me. *Application for Immortality.*

Yes, definitely a joke. Are there hidden cameras somewhere?

But there's nothing else for me to do than fill out this form. He's not giving me any answers, so complying is all I can do. Maybe that will somehow get me out of this strange place. Maybe it's a dream? Is that why everything else is so hazy?

I pinch myself. Nope, probably not a dream.

With a frown, I start filling in the form, hoping that it's worth my time.

First, it's all the basic information about myself: name, date of birth, place of birth, parents, and so on. Then the questions get trickier.

What is your claim to Immortality? Choose from the options you'll find in the Appendix, part I.

I choose *birth or heritage* as the most suitable answer. Having a Goddess as my mother should be a good enough reason.

How will you use your Immortality for the Greater Good?

That makes me think. Is helping look after the Winter Realm a good answer? Or is that just my job?

I scribble down a few sentences about using my position to help all people in the Realm live a prosperous and healthy life. I hope they don't think that too idealistic. Even though I've not been directly involved in politics yet, I know that not everything in the Realm is perfect. There are poor people, there are diseases that can actually kill Guardians, there's corruption and greed. A country - or Realm - can never be perfect, but I'll do my best to get it closer to that goal.

Are you afraid of death?

I blink. Yes. I think I am. Who isn't. If someone came up to me and asked whether I'd want to live or die, I'd say I'd want to live. Of course. And if that someone would then threaten to kill me, I'd be afraid. I'd fight.

I write a small *Yes* on the line, as if I'm trying to hide my answer.

Would you die to save someone else?

Immediately, I think of my men. Storm. Frost. Crispin. Arc. If one of them was in danger and the only way to save them was to die - yes, I'd believe I'd choose to die. I hope I would. It's all good and well to think about it now, but in the actual situation? But yes, I think I really would. I love them too much to see them go.

Yes.

One last question.

What is a good death?

Another hard one. No pain? No tears? No guilt? No humiliation? No long, dragging death but a quick, painless one?

One that I wouldn't regret.

That's quite a vague answer, but I don't even know who's going to read this. If it's the old man in front of me, I don't think he'd actually look at my responses. He'd just put it on some pile of papers, to be forgotten for eternity.

"I'm done."

I hand him the form and he looks at it in surprise.

"That was quick. Now, let me see, what do I do with this again? Ah yes, the test. I'm afraid I can't administer that level of examination, so you will have to see one of my colleagues."

"There are more of you?" I blurt out and cringe when he looks at me with the air of someone who's just been insulted in the gravest manner.

"You don't assume a library runs itself, surely?" he says, a bit piqued. "Follow me."

He gets up with the sigh of someone who's not walked around for a long time. I wonder if they have regulated working hours here. Holidays? Paid overtime? Somehow, I doubt it. He doesn't look like he's been outside in years.

I follow him out of his little room and along the corridor, around a few corners, past a row of doors that I could swear weren't there before, until we reach a very large red door. It's more of a gate, really.

"I'll leave you to it. Return to me once you're done."

He shuffles off, leaving me alone.

I knock on the door and am surprised when someone knocks back on it from the other side. Is that my signal to enter? I carefully open the door and am almost crushed by a giant hand swinging towards me.

The biggest woman I've ever seen is staring at me, her fist extended in the air, ready to strike the door (and me). She must be a giant, there's no other way for her to be this... big. She's about three times as tall as me, and several times as wide. She'd be pretty if her features weren't skewed somehow, as if they melted and then froze again. Her sleek black hair reaches her waist where a large belt shows off her figure. Several rings of keys hang from it, dangling with every movement she makes.

"Who are you?" she asks with a booming voice. I'm sure it's her normal volume but to me it's as if she's screaming.

"Ehm... I'm here to be tested for Immortality." I've never felt more stupid. What kind of sentence is that. And I can't even refer to the man who brought me here because he never told me his name.

"Oh, I've not had one of you in ages. Come on in," she says cheerfully and I have to fight against the urge to cover my ears. They should provide ear muffs for visitors.

For every step that she takes, I need to walk four. The room is more of an arena, large and round. The floor is covered in sand, but there are no stands and seats around it. There's a giant chair at the other end of it, where the giantess now leads me. She plumps down on her seat and grins at me.

"What's your name, race and age?"

I clear my throat. Let's do this properly.

"I'm Wynter, Daughter of Beira and Heiress to the Winter Throne. I am half Goddess, half Guardian, and turned twenty-two last month."

"Pleased to meet you, Wynter. I am Eithne, your assessor. If you're really the daughter of a Goddess, this is only really a formality, but as you may have noticed, they take formalities very seriously here."

She winks and I have to grin. I know exactly what she means.

"To prove that you are ready to become Immortal, you will need to pass three tests. One physical, one mental and one magical. Which one would you like to start with?"

Physical strength is what I don't have, so I should probably do that first. That way, I still have mental energy. If that makes sense. No, it probably doesn't.

"What happens if I fail the tests?"

"Then you die, just as you were supposed to. No rebirth, no Immortality. You'll stay here or pass on, but you won't return back to the living."

I gulp. She makes it sound like I'm really dead.

I take a deep breath. "How did I die?"

She frowns. "Did nobody tell you? You were poisoned with the venom of a black dragon. I didn't think they still existed, but it looks like someone found one and either killed it or forced it to give up some of its venom. In either case, they must be incredibly powerful to do such a feat."

I swallow hard. Someone poisoned me. I'm dead.

The room begins to spin and I have to blink several times to get a grip on reality. Don't faint. Don't cry. Just be strong, Wyn, do these tests and then go home. To my men. Oh Gods. They must be furious. Or grieving. Or both.

"Does time pass the same way here as in the Realms?"

Eithne smiles at me. "That's an excellent question. It depends on the Realm, but I believe the Winter Realm is aligned closely to the Library, so there shouldn't be much difference. Maybe a few minutes less, give or take."

"So I've been dead for hours. What's going on with my... body?"

She laughs. "Don't worry, your mother knows what's going on. Beira founded this place, and she still comes here occasionally. I assume the reason she isn't here right now is that she wants you to prove yourself on your own. Now, which test would you like to start with?"

"Physical," I mutter, my head spinning. My mother knows I'm here and didn't come to bring me home? She doesn't want to support me? I hope she at least told my Guardians that I'm not really dead... not yet, anyway.

Chapter Six

The Giantess takes out a massive clipboard and crosses her legs. She seems excited about the tests I'm about to undertake. If only I knew what they were - but I'm about to find out.

"The physical test... well, first, the rules. You may not use magic in any shape or form. You may not leave the room. You may not ask me for help. You may not forfeit. You may kill. You may maim. Understood?"

I nod. "Let's get this over with."

I'm not sure what I was expecting, but it certainly wasn't a ghost to appear in front of me. It's a man, mostly translucent and the rest of him is misty. His features are barely recognisable, so it could pretty much be anyone. But from his general stature, I assume it's a man.

He walks, no, he *floats* towards me, his arms hanging loosely by his side. He doesn't look very threatening.

"Am I supposed to fight him?" I whisper to the Giantess, but she doesn't reply. Looks like I'm on my own.

She said something about killing and maiming. How am I supposed to do that without a weapon? I don't have magic either, so all I have is my own pitifully untrained body. You know how they say, 'I couldn't hurt a fly'? Well, I probably wouldn't be strong enough to. That's how non-sporty I am.

The ghost comes closer and I take a step back when he stretches out his hands. If he touches me, will it hurt? Will I fail the test? I wish Eithne would tell me what to do. I can't just attack a ghost without being provoked. Maybe he just wants to play…

Or not. His misty form suddenly turns bright red and his eyes begin to glow eerily. Now he doesn't look as harmless anymore. His mouth opens and he lets out a wail that makes a cold shiver run over my back. What is he?

I stumble backwards as he becomes faster. He's chasing me now. How am I supposed to fight him? I'm not sure I could even touch him, he looks far too insubstantial for that. My hands would probably go right through his body.

"What do I do?" I shout at the Giantess, but all she does is smile. Arrrggh. Time to change tactics.

"I don't want to hurt you!" I tell the ghost while starting to run. "What do you want from me?"

His wail turns into a long, drawn-out word. "Liiiiiifffeeeeeee."

Oh. That's not a good sign. He wants my life? My life force?

"Not possible. I'm dead, or so they tell me."

He stops. Is his colour becoming slightly less red? Hard to tell.

"Nooooo liiiiffffeeeeee?"

"No life. I was poisoned, so I'm no longer alive."

His shoulders sag and the red colour leaves his misty body until he's almost pure white again. If he had an actual face, I imagine he'd look sad.

"What do we do now?" I ask him, not expecting much of a reply. Wailing is all he seems to be able to do. Poor guy.

"Fiiiiiiiiiight?"

I shake my head determinedly. "No, I don't want to fight you. How about you go back to where you came from?"

"Piiitttyyyyyyyyyyy?"

"You want me to pity you?"

"Yeeesssssss."

"Ehm, okay. I pity you. I wish you weren't a ghost who had to get life from others."

I hope that's what he wants to hear. When he stays quiet, I add, "I pity you a lot."

Eithne is trying to hide a chuckle, but with her loud voice, that's nearly impossible.

"Thaaaaaaaank youuuuuuuuuuuu," he wails and pops out of existence.

How very strange.

"What happens now? That was my physical?" I ask my examiner who's still hiding her smile with a hand.

"He's never behaved like that before," she finally says. "He was supposed to touch you, then turn into an opponent that would be a challenge but not unbeatable. To be honest, I'm not quite sure what to do now."

"Skip to the next task?" I ask hopefully and to my great relief, she shrugs.

"It says nowhere in the rules that you'd have to repeat it if the ghost leaves. You've not died, so you've passed the first test."

I smile widely, then remember I have two more to go.

"Would you like to do the magical or mental test next?"

"Mental?"

"Alright, for that one you better sit down. I'd also recommend you keep your barriers up for as long as possible."

I do as she says, wondering about that ominous warning. My mental barriers have become a lot stronger, but Arc is still able to break through occasionally. I don't know how he compares to others though. He's stronger than my other three Guardians, but maybe they're just mentally weak? An image of Storm lifting an eyebrow slips into my mind and I have to smile. No, he's definitely not weak.

I close my eyes and focus on my magic. She didn't say anything about me being not allowed to use it. I nudge my magic to strengthen my mental barriers. The translucent globe around my mind turns a slight rainbow sheen, the sign that it's working as intended. I do a quick check like Arc told me. No holes anywhere, no weak spots. The glass is smooth and strong, and hopefully impenetrable.

I smile as I remember the first time I learned how to do this. Arc tried to make me lower my barriers by pretending to be in danger – and it worked. He managed to get in easily, and then took away my clothes. Yes, that was fun. But I've learned my lesson. Whatever I will see isn't real, and I won't let anyone in, no matter who. I'm not going to be that stupid again.

My parents appear on the other side of my barrier, screaming.

Oh no.

My mother's usually perfect hair is tousled and standing in all directions. There's soot on both of their faces and their clothes are smouldering in several places. My father's glasses are cracked and there's a deep, bleeding gash on his forehead. Blood is running down his face and neck, staining his white shirt. What happened to them?

"Mum! Dad!" I shout, fighting to keep a hold on the barrier that every instinct in me is telling me to drop. My parents are in danger and I can help them. I need to.

My heart is fighting my mind. It's not real. It has to be. But what if it is? What if they need help? What if they will die if I don't lower my barriers? What if...

They're starting to beat their hands against the glass dome, my dad's leaving bloody handprints. They want to come in. Their mouths are forming words that I can't understand, but it's clear that they're desperate.

What am I going to do?

My rational mind takes over for a moment and my thoughts become less frantic. What if... yes, that could work. I won't need to lower my barriers if I extend them, enclosing my parents.

But I've never done it before, is it even possible? And is moving it or making it bigger easier? I'll try moving first.

I take a deep breath and coax my magic out of her cave. I need all the power I can access if this is to succeed.

Another deep breath. Then I stretch out my hands and imagine pushing the barrier forwards, away from me. I'm standing in the middle of my dome, so even if I move it a little, I will still be inside. It's big enough for me to do several steps in all directions; right now I'm glad I made it this large when I first created it.

The barrier is resisting, it doesn't want to move. But it has to. I push as hard as I can. Pain is making its way into my temples but I ignore it. Push. PUSH.

Finally, it begins to move. Slowly, only the width of a hair, but it's moving. It proves that it's possible.

I draw more magic into my movement and will the barrier to shift.

It gets faster, but not any easier. Sweat is running down my face and my head is getting more and more painful. I won't be able to keep this up for much longer.

My parents' hands press against the barrier, but now that it's moving, they are slowly being sucked in. It's not breaking the barrier, it's as if it suddenly becomes elastic in those places, taking in my parents without letting anything else in. Like a membrane that is programmed to only accept certain things.

I smile when I see that their hands are fully in. Keeping my grasp firmly on the barrier, I run forward, grasping my mothers' wrists, pulling her to me. With a squelching sound, the dome lets her in and she falls into my arms, making me stumble backwards in surprise. We crash to the floor, her on top of me, and we're laughing and crying at the same time. My mother is here with me. My mum.

I jump up and pull my father in as well. He gives me a shaky hug.

"Well done, Wyn," he whispers into my ear, then he's gone.

They're both gone, as if they were never here. But the smell of smoke and singed fabric still hangs in the air, telling me that it was at least partly real.

I take a deep breath, relief flooding me. I saved them without lowering my barriers. The pain in my head slowly dissipates until it's only a small ache behind my temples.

I did it.

"Well done," Eithne's voice breaks through my concentration. I open my eyes and look at the smiling giantess. "I wasn't sure at first if you'd be able to resist temptation, and I guess in the end, you didn't, but you found a solution." She clears her throat. "Not sure I've ever seen anyone do that before. It was a good solution, though, so you've passed the test."

I sigh in relief. Two down, one more to go. The final task will be magical. I've left the easiest till last. Everybody's constantly telling me how strong my magic is, so this shouldn't be a problem for me.

My magic meows loudly in protest. Okay then. I admit, she's been a little troublemaker recently. I've lost control of her not just once. But surely she's interested in helping me now? If I die, she dies. I think. Nobody knows really, at least I haven't found anything about it in the books in the Palace library. I read quite a few of them to find out why my magic is so much more autonomous than other people's. Mine has a personality, hell, she's even got her own rainbow cave inside of me. She looks like a cat and meows – maybe it's just a sign of my craziness? Or is she different, unique? My mother couldn't help me either; as the Mother of Gods and one of the first beings in existence, magic has always been instinctive for her. She wills things to happen and they do as they're told.

She doesn't have to find a connection to the elements to use their intrinsic magic, she just thinks of setting something on fire and it happens. It was depressing to hear how easy it all is for her. Pity that kind of control of magic wasn't passed on to me.

She said my father wasn't very magically gifted, so I suppose I should be grateful that I'm as strong as I am. I've not pieced together the entire story, but from what my mother and Tamara told me, Beira created my father because she was lonely. I was never planned.

I shake off those thoughts and concentrate on the task at hand.

The giantess is watching me closely. "Everything okay?"

I nod. "I'm ready."

She smiles and points towards the centre of the circular room. "You may want to get up and ready yourself. This may be more of a challenge than you think."

Her knowing smile tells me that she knows more about me than I'd like her to. Am I becoming arrogant? I certainly hope not.

I walk a few steps until I'm more or less in the centre. Somehow, I feel vulnerable. If I had a wall at my back, I wouldn't have to be aware of who might attack me from behind. But it's clear Eithne wants me to be in this position, so I stay, readying myself.

I firmly grip my hold on my magic, ready to throw up a barrier should someone throw something at me. The strongest element in the room is earth, with air being a close second. No water or fire, sadly, those are the ones I feel most confident in. Although my control over air has improved a lot and I'm now able to pick up smaller objects without destroying everything around them. Most of the time. If my magic isn't throwing a tantrum.

Nothing is happening and with every second that passes, I'm getting more and more nervous. To distract myself, I let two little whirlwinds form above my hands, turning quickly around their own axis. Creating them doesn't take much thought or energy anymore, especially not here where the room is saturated with air magic. Wind isn't always the best defence, but it can be great offence and a way to restrain your opponent.

"Nervous?" Eithne chuckles and I'm tempted to throw one of the baby tornados into her direction. She's friendly, but I'm not quite sure yet if I like her. She's enjoying this a little too much, not caring that her tests might end in my death. Or loss of Immortality. Whatever.

Still, everything stays quiet. My feeling of unease is increasing. Is this part of the test? Seeing how I cope under pressure? Well, I've got my Princess mask on and I don't think anyone would see my nervousness. Except for the giantess, apparently. I'm pretty sure by now that she's telepathic. She picks up too many things for it to be coincidence.

Finally, there's a noise behind me and I swirl around, ready to throw the air magic at them. Except that it's my mother.

Beira is here.

My heart drops. I'll never win against a Goddess, let alone her. She's the most powerful of them all. And I wouldn't want to hurt her anyway, not after experiencing her almost being murdered a few weeks ago.

"Hello, my daughter," she says in a cold voice, so unlike the Beira I've got to know. It's like she's talking to someone far beneath her who's angered her. Someone she's going to punish for their crimes. I've only been to one court session so far but that was exactly the way she sounded there. Cold, detached, regal.

"Mother," I respond warily. "Why are you here?"

"You died. I'm making sure you stay dead." Her face is a mask of ice, her eyes dark spheres without any spark of sympathy or love.

"You can't mean that," I splutter, backing away from her approaching form. "You're not yourself."

She smiles mirthlessly. "Oh, I'm certainly myself. I've been waiting for this moment ever since you were born. I can finally get rid of you and erase the mistake I made. Without you, the memory of your father will fade and I can once again be the Queen I was before I created him. Don't worry, I'll make it quick."

She raises her hands and icicles sprout from her fingers. It looks like she's growing claws.

I stumble backwards, tears running down my face. What she said... is it true? Was it all a farce? But...

She throws an icicle at me and I just about manage to expand one of my mini tornados in front of me to build a barrier. The icicle falls to the ground and breaks into a million pieces.

My mother laughs cruelly. "Don't prolong it, Wynter. You can't escape your destiny."

In response, I draw on my earth magic and rip open the floor, turning the tiles into a mound in front of me. It's not much of a barrier, but at least it may act as a distraction.

"Why are you doing this?" I shout again, deflecting one of her icicles with another bout of wind. She's throwing them at me quicker and quicker, and I'm noticing how my energy is waning already. I don't even have the time to mount a counterattack, all I do is defend myself. But I'm aware she is holding back. She could crush me with a single thought. Right now, she is toying with me.

Almost lazily, she flicks another icicle into my direction. This time, I throw some earth up into the air, blocking it. The icicle and the ball of sand it's stuck in fall to the ground. There's no time to rest. I crouch down on the floor, hiding behind my barrier so that I only have to protect my upper body from her assault.

It's not until pain races through my back that I notice my mistake. I thought in human terms, not in magical. In this world, icicles don't have to fly in a straight line. They can circle and approach from behind... like this one just did.

I fall onto my belly, my back muscles spasming. I feebly try and get up, but my legs aren't working. She's got me incapacitated after mere minutes of fighting. Demons were child's play compared to this. I have no chance against my mother. It was stupid to even try.

Suddenly, she's by my side, drawing a cold finger over my cheek. It stings and I move to get out of her reach, but I'm too weak. The tremors in my back are making their way into my shoulders until my arms start to shake. I still have access to my magic though. I ask her to connect to the air around me and she does it without any further nudging. For once, she does what I'm asking her to.

With air magic surrounding me from all sides, I manage to sit up, propped up against the air that is now feeling almost solid. At least this way, I can look my death into the eyes.

My mother.

Her expression is cold, unfeeling. Was it all an act? All the chats we had, all the laughter? Did she just pretend to be the person I thought she was?

A tear runs down my cheek, in the same place where she touched me just a moment ago. She's breaking my heart but doesn't seem to care. If only my Guardians were here. But then I remember how strong she is and am glad they aren't. She'd likely kill them without a second thought.

I want to say something, but I know it will only look I'm begging her for my life. I don't want to give her that satisfaction. So I stay silent, looking into her dark eyes... wait, doesn't she have blue eyes? As bright as snowflakes on a crisp day? Then why do they look like coals, smouldering with hate?

"You aren't Beira," I whisper, hoping that I'm right. "You're not my mother."

She smiles. "No, I'm not. But I'm glad you thought I was. What does that tell you about your relationship with your mother?"

She steps back and a massive icicle grows from her fingers. It's clearly intended to stab me through my heart.

But now that I know she isn't Beira, I also know she's not as strong as I thought. Maybe she hasn't been playing with me after all. Maybe that was the extent of her power. Which is strong, definitely, but perhaps I can still fight her. She's not my mother, so if I hurt her, I don't care. Whoever she is, she's my enemy.

My mind clears and I let my emotions drift away. All that counts now is surviving.

Ignoring the pain in my back, I grab a hold on the air around me and propel myself away from the Beira impostor until I'm at the other end of the room with the wall at my back. No more sneak attacks from behind. I'm finding it hard to keep my grip on the air holding me in place while gathering fire magic. She's only used icicles so far, which gives me some hope. Maybe that's all she can do.

Trying to hide my intentions, I use more air magic to deflect the icicles she's started throwing my way again. I'm now doing three things at once and my energy is waning fast. I will have to be quick and defeat her while I still can.

Finally, I've got enough fire gathered. I release it not in front of me like I usually would before sending it in someone's direction in the shape of a fireball.

No, this time, I conjure the fire around fake-Beira, trapping her in a column of fire. She screams as flames touch her skin. She seems unable to escape her fiery prison, no matter how much ice she throws at it. I increase the temperature of the fire and draw it closer, until there's no space between her and the flames.

Her screams become louder as the fire burns her. I have to look away as smoke begins to fill the air above and her shrieks start to fade.

I just burned someone alive.

When I'm sure she's gone, I let the flames fizzle out and drop to the ground. Pain floods my mind. Now that I'm no longer having to fight, the pain is overwhelming me.

"Well done," Eithne says softly, kneeling down by my side. She puts her large hands on my back and I flinch, expecting more pain, but strangely enough, the agony lessens at her touch. She rubs her hands back and forth and with every move, I'm feeling better. The tingles in my legs stop and I'm able to move my toes again.

When she gets up again, I'm feeling well again. No pain. Even my energy is back to where it was before the fight started. It's as if nothing happened, but the pile of ash in the centre of the room tells a different story.

I scramble to my feet.

"Well done," Eithne repeats. "You've passed the tests. You can go back to the clerk now and he'll give you your Immortality certificate."

"Just like that?"

It's a bit of an anti-climax. I kill someone and she tells me to go back to the old man with his folders and stacks of paper?

"Do you want to repeat one of the tests?" she asks drily and I immediately shake my head. No, thanks. That was enough. I'm mentally exhausted and am sure this whole experience is going to give me nightmares for weeks to come. Especially the things my mother said... No, let's not dwell on that. The priority is to get out of here, preferably alive.

"I can't come with you for obvious reasons, but I'm sure you'll find your way back, right?"

She points at her large form and I remember how narrow some of the corridors were. Does that mean she lives in this room? It's the only one with a door big enough to let her in and out.

What a strange place. One I'll be glad to leave.

T he clerk is bent over some files, mumbling to himself. I clear my throat several times until he finally looks up.

"Oh, you again. Yes?"

I sigh. "I passed the tests, can I go home now?"

He hands me another form. What a surprise.

"I just need a signature here… and here… and on this one…"

After I've signed at least ten documents, he pushes up his glasses and gathers some of the files into a pile.

"All seems to be in order. You've achieved Immortality, congratulations. You will now be transported back to the place of your death."

"Ehm, thank you," I mutter, not really sure about what to say.

Then I see the book on his desk and remember that I filled in a form earlier to borrow it.

"But what about my book?"

"It will be delivered to you when it's time."

"What?"

The library blinks out of existence.

Chapter Seven

I don't feel different when I wake up. Not like anything has changed. It's as if it all never happened. But the concerned eyes of my four Guardians tell me all I need to know. It was real. Someone killed me. And I'm back, alive, Immortal.

"Wyn, you made it," Crispin whispers, his eyes red-rimmed. "I... " His voice fails and he stifles a sob. I tear up watching him being so emotional. He must have thought I was dead. Judging from their exhausted expressions, they all have.

"See, I told you she would make it."

My mother makes her way to my bed and the twins step away respectfully, their gaze still fixed on me. They seem too shocked to speak.

"Wyn, I am so proud of you." Beira presses a soft kiss on my forehead. Her skin is surprisingly warm. When she pulls back, I quickly check her eyes. Blue, thank the Gods. Not black like that nightmare Beira I had to fight.

"I knew you would get out of there, but still... well done."

She turns to leave but stops before reaching the door. "Now stop whining, boys, and find whoever did this."

My Guardians snap to attention.

"Yes, your Highness," Storm says with a small bow. Only because I know him so well can I see that he's only pretending to be so calm. There's a slight tremor to the hands he's got pressed against his sides and his brow is a little more furrowed than usual.

My mother sweeps out of the room and I'm finally alone with my men. They no longer hold back. Suddenly I'm held by all four of them and the comfort they give me is just what I need now, even if I didn't realise it. I may be okay physically, but that doesn't mean that my experience in the Library hasn't left any marks on me mentally. I fought my mother, after all, even though she turned out to be fake. I heard what she said. I burned her alive.

Hands rub my back and I revel in the warmth they all give me.

"I missed you," I whisper but Frost's mouth on my lips stops me from saying anything more. He kisses me gently, as if he's afraid that I might disappear again. But I'm here to stay, and I show him by deepening the kiss, hungrily sucking on his bottom lip. These men are mine and I'm not going to leave them alone.

Frost slips his hands under my shirt, but it's not long until one of the others lifts my arms and pulls the garment over my head. It's a pity I have to break the kiss for that. I'm not wearing anything underneath, and I'm very aware that the only clothing I have left are my panties. That's what Storm put me in when I went to sleep after our date. It feels so long ago already.

Arc takes Frost's place, his lips a lot rougher than the other Guardian's. He pulls me closer until I sit on his lap. There's something hard waiting for me there. But there's no time to even think about it before my mind is fully occupied with Arc's demanding kiss. Hands are rubbing over my back, cupping my breasts, caressing my skin. So many sensations...

I moan against Arc's mouth which he takes as an invitation to nibble on my bottom lip. I fight him off with my tongue, which he meets with his own. We kiss and kiss while others touch me, while my Guardians explore my body. My skin tingles everywhere and I'm afraid I might faint from all the feelings. Not just physical, emotional as well. All four of them are here with me. I'm not dead, on the contrary, I'm now Immortal. I'll be able to spend all my life with them. All my never-ending life.

"What are ye thinking?" Arc whispers and I only now realise I stopped our kiss.

"I'm happy," is all I can come up with, but from the sparkle in his eyes, I can see how he knows exactly what I mean. We're in this together. All five of us. My beautiful, amazing Guardians.

Arc gives me a gentle kiss on the lips, as if he's not quite sure whether I want to continue. But of course I do. I return the kiss, showing him that it's okay, that I want him to be passionate and demanding again. I like it when his lips are hard on mine. Almost rough.

I slip one hand between us, touching his cock through the thick fabric of his jeans. He must be aching in there, surrounded by such a constricting prison. I fumble with his button and zip until he's finally in my hand. His silky skin is smooth as I rub his erection. He groans and breaks the kiss, leaning back a little to give me better access. I climb off his lap to make it easier for him to slip out of his jeans. That's when I notice that the other three have already done that. Even Crispin is naked and ready for me.

He looks unsure though, his expression hard to read. Is he okay with this? Is he just doing it to make me happy?

So far, he's never stayed when there was any kind of physical action between me and the others. But now, he's here and judging from his hardness, he wants me just as much as I want him. But will the ghosts plaguing him let him?

I slide off the bed and walk towards him, seeking his gaze. His blue eyes capture mine, giving me the confidence to run my hands over his naked chest. His muscles are hard and defined, even though he's the smallest of the guys. He's not as broad as Arc and not as strong as the twins, but he's still perfect to me. I explore his skin, moving my fingers over his chest, then his back. I step closer when I reach his buttocks until I feel the tip of his cock on my belly.

"Wyn," he groans, "I'm not sure this is a good idea."

I want to tell him that it is, but I know how hard this must be for him. I don't want to make it any harder.

"We'll only go as far as you want, Crisp," I reassure him. "Don't worry about it."

"But I do worry," he says huskily. "I worry that if I start, I won't be able to let go of you."

"Then don't let go..."

He ends my sentence with a kiss. He's gentle, tentative almost. It feels like a dream, not quite real, but believable. I'm finally kissing my blond Guardian. The one who's tried to stay distant for so long.

My Crispin.

I pull him closer, squeezing his bum until there's no more room between us. Skin on skin, lips on lips. Our kiss is getting more desperate, both of us gasping for air as our connection grows. We're drowning in each other, not knowing where one of us begins and the other ends.

His mind is touching mine and I open my barriers to him, letting him in. With our bodies and our minds entwined, him sliding his cock into me is only natural. He carries me to the bed, not leaving the warmth of my core, and lays me down on the cool silk.

I feel the others watching us as he begins to move in me, carefully letting me get used to him being inside me. He's a perfect fit, not too small, not too big, just right.

I can't believe this is our first time. It doesn't feel like it. It's like we've been together for years, him and me and the others. It's normal. And beautiful.

He leans down to kiss me again while jerking his hips faster and faster. I'm getting closer to coming, but I don't want to yet. I need to be with him longer, I don't want him to stop. I close my eyes and focus on the sensations. The others take that as an invitation to touch my body again. Someone is massaging my breasts while another is trailing soft kisses along my belly. I moan and grip the bedsheets tightly, needing something to hold on to.

The others are caressing my skin, but they are holding back at the same time, giving Crispin the space he needs. If it was one of the others, they'd be all over me and probably in me. We've done that before. But right now, it's almost as if Crispin and I were alone.

His thrusts are getting more erratic and I'm getting ever closer to that sweet point I'm sailing towards. I reach up and pull him closer, wanting to touch him when we come apart. He obliges, turning me onto the side while lying down next to me, until we're looking into each other's' eyes. He captures my gaze as my moans are getting louder and I'm beginning to quiver uncontrollably. We're almost there... Almost. Just one more push...

We merge and become one. As our bodies unite, our minds meet in an explosion of colour. I see him, Crispin, the real Crispin behind the mask. I can see his darkness, his sorrow, his wounds. I want to reach out and make them all go away, heal him from the inside out, but I know that's not possible. I file the information away for later; I need to help him deal with all that darkness. No wonder he's been holding back.

Somehow, I know that while I'm looking into him, he's doing the same to me. He will see things I'm trying to keep hidden. Will he be overwhelmed? Will he turn away in disgust when he sees what I'm like?

I pull away, giving him his privacy, hoping that he will do the same.

A moment later, I'm back in my body as if nothing happened. My body is shaking from the orgasm that is still running through me, strong and sweet. Overwhelming. Magnificent.

Frost suddenly cries out and I'm ripped out of my dreamy state.

"Wyn, get those things out of my face!"

I turn and see my wings fully expanded, shimmering in the air, almost pulsating in the heat of the moment. Frost is holding his cheek and I can see a bloody line between his fingers. I hurt him. Oh Gods, I hurt him while I had sex. Again.

It's as if someone's thrown cold water over me. I've messed up. Again.

I try to detangle myself from Crispin, but he holds me tight, not letting me go.

"Don't leave," he whispers. "Frost is okay, right?"

The Guardian in question nods, but there's still blood on his cheek. Having sex shouldn't result in injuries. I'm a terrible girlfriend.

"Sweetie, dinnae be sad." Arc plumps down on the bed beside me, putting one large arm around my naked shoulders. Only now do I notice that my wings have disappeared again. Stupid things. Why do they always get in the way? It's the same with my magic - can't I have a life without them interfering? If I have sex with my Guardians, I want it to be just us, no magic, no funny business. Just a woman and... several men having fun.

I sigh. "I guess that's the end of this evening."

"The end? Nah, it's only just beginning."

Arc pulls me closer until I'm almost on his lap. Crispin still has an arm around my waist, so it feels like I'm being hugged from two sides. It's a good feeling, really.

"Now smile, Princess. Smile fer me."

Arc waits until I dutifully lift the corners of my mouth - I'm not sure how convincing it is - then he kisses me gently. It's a reassuring, kind sort of kiss, not one in the heat of the moment. He's trying to comfort me, and he's succeeding. Ironically, it should be Frost who should be comforted. He's the injured one, not me. But Arc kissing Frost... I'm not sure they're into that kind of thing. Although it would be pretty hot to watch...

I feel my nipples tighten and apparently, I'm not the only one who's noticing that. Storm kneels down on the bed in front of me and takes one of them into his mouth, sucking hard. I gasp and arch my back, supported by my other two Guardians. Frost is still standing next to the bed, but his eyes are dilated as he watches Storm play with my breasts.

He licks his lips, then gives me a wide grin.

"To make up for it, I think it should be my turn now."

He stalks towards the foot end of the bed and spreads my legs, gently running his hands along my bare thighs. They are cool on my flushed skin, giving me goosebumps. Together with Storm's fingers twirling my nipples and Arc kissing me passionately, my arousal is reaching new heights. Crispin is lying by my side, hugging me around the waist, comfortable in the knowledge that we've seen each other's darkness and have not been pulled apart by it. Something happened, something I need to explore. I thought we were already bonded, but this feels even stronger, almost tangible.

Frost enters me and my world falls apart.

I'm with my Guardians and they are with me. What else could I want?

When he makes me come, I know that this is heaven. And when the others get involved, it turns into paradise.

There's a loud knock on the door and I lazily lift my head. Only one person in the Palace would dare to knock on the Princess's door in that way.

"What do you want, Tamara?"

"Council meeting in ten minutes!" she shouts back. A chorus of groans from the guys around me accompany her announcement.

"Do we have ta?" Arc grumbles and pulls the blanket over his head. He doesn't just hide though, no, he begins to suckle on one of my nipples. I push him away with a pang of regret.

"Not now, we need to go."

"But I dinnae want ta," he complains, this time squeezing my other breast with his hand.

With a deep sigh, I remove his hand. The woman in me wants him to be there, but the Heiress in me knows that I have responsibilities.

"Touching my boobs won't make me change my mind."

He surfaces from under the duvet and grins. "How about touching you here?"

His thumb rubs over my bud, still swollen from earlier. I moan involuntarily.

"Stop it," Storm tells him, "she's right, we need to go."

Arc groans loudly. "I hate being a Guardian."

I chuckle. "Believe me, I'd rather be a Guardian than a Demigoddess with weird powers."

Frost pulls me out of bed and gives me a gentle kiss. "I like your powers. Although you really have to work on your wing control." He rubs his cheek, still red from where my wings hit him.

"Sorry," I mumble, embarrassment making me blush.

"Don't be. It's cute when you do stuff like that. Remember how you set me on fire?"

As if I could forget. Frost was giving me a lesson in how to control water which somehow turned into a making out session. Which I ended in the heat of the moment by becoming a little too hot. I lost control of my magic and set him on fire. Back then, he didn't find it as funny; he must have been in terrible pain. But apparently, we've reached the stage where we can joke about it.

Crispin, already fully dressed, hands me some clothes. I would love to have a shower but there's no time. After. Maybe with a Guardian or two. Luckily, my bathroom here is bigger than my entire room back at my parents' house on Earth.

That reminds me... only a few more days until I can try and contact them. So much has happened that I almost forgot. Does that make me a bad daughter? I suppose so. But I kind of died so that should be a good excuse.

Arc is the last to get up, still grumbling and complaining, but at least he hurries to put on some clothes. I can't wait to undress him later. My Guardians are not made for wearing clothes.

Chapter Eight

All of the important members of my mother's Court are already seated in the council chamber, waiting for us. I straighten my back and take a seat at Beira's side, ignoring their curious glances. Storm sits down next to me, while the other three take position behind my chair. On the way here, Storm explained that usually they're not part of the Council, but that my mother specifically requested their presence.

This is only the second Council session I'm attending. The first was to introduce me to my mother's advisors and to tell me that I would be given some time to adjust to life in the Realm before taking on more official duties. That was fine with me, but it looks like now the time has come to get involved in the running of the country.

Tamara is the only one not sitting around the large mahogany table, instead, she's on a basic chair behind my mother. It's strange how even in these important meetings, she's still pretending to be less important than she really is. Without her, Beira would have a hard time running the place. Tamara is the spy mistress, the head of intelligence and my mother's most trusted advisor all at the same time. But not many people know that; they just know her as the Mistress of the Household, the woman dealing with the everyday affairs of the Palace. If only they knew she's so much more than that...

She winks at me and I instantly feel more at ease.

Next to Storm sits Ada, the Guardian who welcomed me to the Realm when we first arrived at the Gate. It's strange seeing her on her own, usually she's always surrounded by her three colleagues and lovers. It's good to know that I'm not the only one with multiple partners - although of course there is a lot of gossip about it making the rounds. Tamara regularly tells me the juiciest bits of gossip floating through the Palace. It's become a good source of entertainment for the guys and me. Compared to what people think of us, we're actually really innocent. After all, today was the first time we all slept together. Not that we did much sleeping. We were busy doing... other things.

There are a few more familiar faces around the table. Theodore the healer, who I met at the beginning when my magic was locked away. I'm not sure I like him very much; his arrogance is overpowering. I'm glad Jonathan, the Lord Chamberlain, isn't here, his ego is even bigger than Theodore's.

Gwain is the Master of Arms and Ada's superior. I think Storm reports to him as well, if he doesn't get direct commands from my mother. He's an imposing man whose age doesn't detract from his strength but adds to it. A scar across his left eyebrow tells stories of battles and narrow escapes. He's a harsh man, but I like him. He says what he thinks which is a welcome contrast to most of the other Council members.

Like Magnus, the Treasurer. He'd lick my mother's arse if it would result in something positive for him. It's clear that he's interested in more power for him, but I think he's too timid to act on it. Still, someone to keep an eye on. He's clever though, so I can see why my mother keeps him.

I've not talked to Algonquin, the Royal Librarian, or Zephyr, the Master of the Wings yet. They're both quite old, which I always find surprising for Guardians. Are they made that way? Has Algonquin always looked like a wise old wizard? Or did he age somehow, even though he's immortal?

One day I will have to ask someone about it. Pity I only ever come up with these questions while I don't have an opportunity to ask.

My mother clears her throat and the room instantly quiets.

"Thank you for coming at such short notice. There have been new developments that need immediate action." All eyes are on her, captivated by both her words and her voice that makes you want to listen and do whatever she says.

"My daughter, Wynter, has achieved Immortality."

The room erupts into noise, but a single snowflake floating down from the ceiling makes them all quiet down immediately. I admire my mother for how she's dealing with the Council. She doesn't even need to use words to keep them under control. A snowflake is enough to make them shut up. Wow.

But from their stares, I know that they're all thinking the same thing. If I am now Immortal, I died before reaching that state. And as I was in perfect health before, it means someone killed me. I shudder at the thought that mere hours ago, I was a lifeless corpse.

"We have a suspect in custody. They used poison, but we have yet to establish how. Wyn, do you have any information that could help?"

"No, all I remember is waking up and not feeling well. There was someone in my room, but I didn't see his features. He said something like 'I am Death', but he never touched me. I think. I passed out before I could call for help."

"I felt her distress," Storm says quietly, the torment of the memory evident in his voice. "She was dead by the time we got to her room. It must have been incredibly fast acting."

Theodore stands and bows to the Queen. "When I examined her, there were faint traces of magic in the room, but none on her body. I don't think she was... killed," he clears his throat and looks at me uncomfortably, "by means of magic. It must have been normal poison."

"Nothing about this is normal," Frost hisses from behind me, but a stern look from Storm shuts him up.

"You are right, Guardian," my mother says loudly. "This assassin should never have made it into my daughter's bedroom. Neither should she have been alone."

She gives Storm a pointed glance and I almost think he's blushing. Of course my mother knows. She knows everything, and if she doesn't, then Tamara does.

"I only left for half an hour," Storm defends himself. "So either she was given the poison during that time and it killed her within those thirty minutes, or it was administered earlier and took some time to act. I was with the Princess all day so I don't think that's the correct theory. Unless... we ate together. Maybe it was in the food?"

"Gwain, ask Merrill whether there are any new people working in the kitchens," Beira commands and the Master of Arms nods in agreement. I feel bad for Merrill, the cook. She's a lovely person, always ready to give me a massive hug and a piece of cake. She's one of those naturally huggy people.

"Ada, I want you to interrogate the suspect. He's likely still unconscious, so take Theodore with you to make sure he gets into a state where we can question him."

"Yes, your Majesty," Ada agrees, turning to the healer. "Why is he unconscious?"

"He took poison when we captured him. Luckily, I was nearby and managed to lessen the effect. He will survive, but he will wish he did not in the next few hours. He will be in a lot of pain."

"Good," Ada says passionately. It surprises me, usually I know her as a very composed person. Is she really upset about that assassin trying to kill me? If she is, she's just jumped up in my list of people I can trust in the Palace.

My mother folds her hands, seemingly calm, but I can see she isn't. I've come to know her well enough to see behind the icy mask she wears in public. Inside, she's really quite an emotional person, even though she'd never admit that.

"Storm, I want at least two of you with Wyn at any time from now on. Don't let her out of your sight. She may be Immortal now, but we all know that there are still ways she can be killed."

Yes, we know. The Summer King almost managed to kill Beira a few weeks ago, and if he has weapons capable of that, it's easy to believe that he can kill me if he can get close to me. Or his assassins. I don't think he's the type to actually do the dirty work himself.

"Do you think it was Angus?" I ask and all eyes are on my mother. The Summer King has been very active recently, so it's likely.

Beira doesn't say anything for a moment, only frowns. Then she says hesitantly, "It certainly looks like it. It would be an easy answer. But there is one thing that doesn't make sense. Gwain, show them what you found in the corridor outside Wyn's room."

Gwain stands and holds up a small thing for all to see. It's blue and shiny, but I can't quite make out what it is.

"Is that a scale?" Zephyr asks, speaking for the first time.

"Yes, it is. Take a look." Gwain hands it to the Master of the Wings and Zephyr investigates it closely.

"I don't believe this..."

"Would you enlighten the rest of us?" Theodore asks impatiently and for once, I agree with him.

"It's a dragon scale. The scale of an ice dragon, if I'm not mistaken."

The room breaks into noise. This time, my mother needs to shout "Silence!" for them all to shut up.

"I know it's worrying. The ice dragons are our allies, at least that's what we were thinking. Algonquin, are you still in contact with their ambassador?"

The librarian nods. "I got a letter from him two weeks ago. He didn't mention anything of importance, but I'm going to read it again, and the ones before. Shall I invite him to Court?"

My mother smiles coolly. "No, not invite. Summon him, order him to appear before me. Even if the dragons don't have anything to do with the assassination attempt, I need to know why one of them was in my Palace."

"Of course, my lady."

"And while you're at it, work with Theodore to find out more about what poison they may have used. Even if the suspect tells us, I want to make sure you can verify his answers."

I suddenly remember something. "When I was dead... ehm, I mean in the Library, the man there said it was the venom of a black dragon that poisoned me."

Zephy gasps. "But they're extinct!"

"Obviously not," my mother says coolly. "Now we have two leads that are both pointing towards the dragons being involved somehow. Algonquin, I want everything you have on black dragon venom summarised by tomorrow." She looks around the room. "Anything else?"

I hesitantly clear my throat.

"Yes, Wyn?"

"This may be a stupid question, but why would anybody want to kill me? I know I'm the Heiress to the throne, but it's not like I have a lot of influence or power. You're the one in charge, shouldn't they target you... again?"

My mother gives me a small smile. "Meet me in my sitting room after this. We have to talk."

She turns to the rest of the Council.

"You're dismissed. We will meet again tonight so everybody

can report their findings. Hopefully, Ada will have managed to talk to the prisoner by then."

My mother is sitting by the fire, looking into the flames, deep in thought. I take a seat on the armchair opposite, holding my hands towards the warming fire. It's a bit cool in here, but that's normal for my mother's quarters. It helps remind people that she is the Winter Queen.

"Did you know I can't feel the warmth of the fire?" she asks suddenly.

"No. Not even if you touch it?"

"Watch." She stretches out a hand until the flames can almost reach her, but the closer she gets, the further they back away, as if they're afraid to be touched. My mother's hand is now in the centre of the fireplace, with the flames flickering weakly in a wide circle around it. They look close to dying completely.

"Wow. Can you do fire magic?"

"No, it's one of the few elements that resist me. But don't tell anyone." She chuckles. "I want them to think that I'm all powerful."

I laugh. "But you are, there's not much you can't do."

Her smile disappears. "Apparently, I can't even protect my daughter in my own Palace. I'm sorry, Wyn. This should never have happened. I thought you were safe now that you are here with me. I didn't think anybody would be as brazen as to try and poison you."

I shrug. "It's not your fault. I'm kind of getting used to people wanting to kill me."

"But you shouldn't have to. I brought you here because you were in danger on Earth. I never thought you'd be in just as much danger in my Realm."

I decide it's time to change the topic. I don't want to think of me being in danger. I quite like living, even though I still need to get used to the whole Immortality thing.

"There's something I wanted to ask you... and you don't need to answer if you don't want to..."

"What is it, Wyn?" my mother asks gently.

"During the trials, after I died... I had to fight you."

"Oh." She laughs. "Was I difficult to beat? I hope you used fire. I may not be able to touch it, but if someone gifted in fire magic throws it at me, I'm having a hard time defending myself against it."

I quickly look at the door, but it's got the familiar yellow glow around it, meaning that nobody can listen in. Of course Beira thought of that. She's a millennia-old Goddess, she is more intelligent and wise than I can even imagine.

"I did use fire, but before that, you said some things... nasty things."

She stops laughing. "What did I say? Don't believe any of it, the Trials are meant to confuse and challenge you, both physically and mentally."

I cringe inside, not knowing how to best approach the subject. In the end, I just blurt it out. "You said that you wanted to kill me because I reminded you of my father. That you want the memory of him to die. Is that true?"

Her face turns even paler than it usually is.

"No, Wyn, I don't want to erase your father's memory. Although I will admit that sometimes it's hard to think of him. He died almost twenty-three years ago, but some days, it's still painful."

I'm tempted to tell her how much I appreciate her honesty, but I don't want to interrupt her.

"Your father was a great man... Guardian. I created him for the wrong reason, and he was quick to tell me that I was wrong. I liked that about him. He wasn't afraid of me like all the others. He said what needed to be said, whether it offended me or not. He was brave, and stupid, sometimes."

She chuckles. "I see a lot of him in you."

This time I can't stay quiet. "You think I'm stupid?"

"Not stupid, brave. A bit rash, sometimes. He showed me how sometimes, it was good to show your emotions. I had been on my own for so long, never trusting anyone, never confiding into anyone. Then he came along and broke through the barriers I had built around myself. Don't ask me how he did it, but even though he was infuriating and stubborn, I fell in love with him."

"And he with you?"

She smiles sadly. "No, I don't think so. That came later. Neither of us told the other what we felt until he was dying. We only had one week together, but that one week was worth all the years of waiting and heartbreak. And that one week gave me you, Wyn, and even though it sometimes hurts, I would never want to lose the memory of your father."

I'm having trouble holding back my tears. She's opened up to me and I feel like I should say something, thank her for it, but I can't find the words. She told me a bit about my father before, that he was a Guardian and that she had created him. But she'd never mentioned their relationship, or that they only spent such a short time together.

We both watch the flames as they crackle and fight for dominance. Even though my mother can't feel the warmth of the fire, I can see why she likes to have a fireplace. It's strangely soothing.

"What else did you have to do during the Trials?" my mother finally asks.

"Stop a ghost from killing me, rescue my parents and kill a Beira impersonator."

Oops. I mentioned my parents. Will she be insulted that I called them that?

"Oh yes, your parents. I know you're trying to contact them... and I approve."

She winks and I stare at her in surprise.

"How do you...?"

But of course I should have known. There's nothing happening in this Realm without Beira knowing. Although there was nobody in the cave besides my Guardians and me. Blaze had left by then. So who told her? Or did she just *know* things?

"Of course I cannot approve of it in public, so you better make sure I don't find out. I think your Guardians call it 'plausible deniability'?"

She shouldn't know that. But I'm not brave enough to ask her how she does. I don't want to become paranoid about what I'm saying to my Guardians in private.

"You better wait a few days though until things have quieted down. There will be several Council sessions I need you to attend. Let's hope that Ada will know more about the assassin tonight, that will make things easier."

She sighs. "I had hoped to spare you from taking a more active part in the affairs of the Realm, but it looks like it wasn't to be. Now that you're part of the Council, they will expect you to attend more often and take an active role. And it will be good to have a fresh voice in there, some of my advisors are rather stuck in their ways."

I can imagine who she's thinking of. And she's right, most of the Council members are old and have probably been in there for centuries or longer. It's hard to tell with Guardians, they never look their actual age. I still haven't persuaded my four Guardians to tell me how old they are. They think it'll make me feel weird about them. Maybe I should just command them. I need practice in playing Princess anyway.

"You were asking earlier about why Angus may want to kill you," my mother begins and I look at her expectantly. That's been playing on my mind for a while.

"To answer that question, I need to give you some background on Angus and me. They call me the Mother of Gods, but for some reason, people don't think of him as the Father. Maybe because he hasn't created as many Gods as I have. He's always thought that having more Gods would decrease the power he holds. He's always been afraid, deeply afraid, that someone might come and usurp him. Even back at the beginning, when it was just him and me, he hated that he wasn't the one in charge. We were made to rule together, but he didn't accept that. He wanted to be the only one. I don't think he's ever not hated me.

"As we could not rule together, we made a pact. I would be in charge for half a year, then him for the other half. That's how I became the Goddess of Winter, and he the God of Summer. We created the Realms, one for each of us. Later, we made more for the Gods we'd created to keep them at peace with each other. And even though we only ruled over life for half a year, we had our own Realm to look after for the other half. Angus should have been happy with that, but of course, he wasn't.

"One year, he refused to pass on the throne to me. By then, it had become such tradition that nature itself was used to it. When Angus ruled, he challenged the plants and animals to grow, to fulfil their potential. When it was my turn, I gave them their well-earned rest, letting them sleep during the winter. Ice and water were thankful when I ruled as they were in permanent danger during summer. It was a balance that should have been preserved... but Angus didn't see it that way.

"He wanted an eternal summer. Luckily, others saw how wrong it was to put the balance of life in jeopardy, so they rebelled. With the help of the other Gods, we managed to push him off the throne so I could resume my rightful rule. When spring came, I was worried that he might do the same thing again, but nonetheless I ended my reign as was custom. I decided to stand above it, to be the better Goddess.

"His rule became more and more violent. Our task was to preserve and create, but he was more interested in being feared by his subjects. He let them starve under scorching heat until everybody had sworn allegiance to him, even some of the lesser Gods. It was easy to see that he was trying to build a following so that next time he challenged me, he would not lose again.

"For a while, we maintained the fragile peace. The seasons turned as they were supposed to and Angus gave the throne to me in the autumn as he was supposed to. Then he met his future wife Bridget and things became difficult once again. She appealed to his jealous side, making him put his plans into action a lot earlier than I think he'd planned. I guess I should have been grateful for it. He wasn't as strong as he could have been, but it was a hard battle nonetheless. I lost a lot of good Gods and Guardians that day. So did he. I know a lot of his followers were coerced into doing his bidding. They didn't actually believe in his vision of an eternal summer. They knew it was wrong, but he had a hold over them so they fought. A few changed allegiance on the battlefield. In the end, we won, but it was not a happy victory."

Beira summons a tray with two cups of tea on the small table between us. I gratefully take a cup, warming my hands on it. She takes a few sips before she continues.

"After that, I managed to keep him in check. He no longer overstepped the barriers, he ruled in the summer like he was supposed to. Grudgingly, and not kind, but he did as he was told. The battle had left him weak and cornered, and even though Bridget kept whispering into his ear, he resisted the temptation of fighting me once again.

"Then, maybe a century ago, I heard reports of him gathering followers again. It's as if he doesn't realise that he can't win. We're equal in power, but only while we keep the balance. His power wanes as soon as he breaks that balance. But he is far too arrogant to see that. His spies have been slipping into my Realm for a long time. We manage to find most of them, but I'm sure there are a few that slip through our nets. There have been a few small attacks... your father was wounded in one of them when Angus tried to capture one of the Gates."

She stops and takes another sip of tea. It must be hard for her to think of that. Angus killed my father, and still she's trying to keep the balance. I admire her for that, I don't think I could do that if someone attacked my Guardians.

"I'm sure he will attack again at some point. For now, he sends assassins and spies, but in the background, he's building an army once more. Past experience has taught him though that he won't be able to win... unless he has something new up his sleeve. And Bridget has convinced him that what he needs is an heir, someone who shares Angus' power and can fight by his side.

"My informants tell me that's he's been trying to create new Gods for a while now, Gods who have his power. But of course that's impossible. We are the original Gods, nobody will ever have the same power we have. His next step was to try have a child with Bridget. It's not been successful. Gods can't have children with each other, no matter how often they try. We can create life from scratch, but we cannot have children like humans can.

"Then I had you. There have been Demigods before, but I don't think either of us thought that Angus or I could have them. It was something the lower Gods did, who were closer in nature to the Guardians they coupled with. But you're the proof that it's possible. And now he's afraid, terribly afraid that you will be able to help me take over his Realm. Of course that's not my aim, it's never been, but Angus is paranoid. It's something he would do if he could, but he can't believe that I don't think in the same way that he does.

"He's been trying to father a Demigod ever since you were born, but as far as I know, he's not managed to do so. It doesn't help that Bridget is extremely jealous and is probably trying to prevent him from sleeping with female Guardians."

She pauses again and I take it as an opportunity to ask questions.

"But do you think it's possible? Him having a child?"

"I'm not sure. Intuition tells me that it's not possible unless there is love. Maybe he and Bridget could even have a child if only they loved each other. But Bridget is with him because of a love for power, not for Angus as a person. And why he is with her... I have no idea. She's quite pretty, but I don't think that's his motivation. So for now, they don't have an heir, and are incredibly jealous that I have you."

"That makes sense... Do you think they will try again?"

"Oh yes." She smiles at me with determination. "But they won't succeed."

Chapter Nine

"He's a dragon," Ada announces to the shocked Council. "He's not said anything but gibberish, but I believe that's due to the pain he's still in. I don't think more violent interrogation methods would do any good at the moment. We need to wait until he's more coherent before we know if he's the assassin. Although everything speaks for it. He left a scale near Wyn's room, he took poison when we captured him, he didn't have any reason to be here."

My mother nods, deep in thought.

"Arc, you're our strongest mindbreaker. Have you taken a look at him?"

"Aye, Yer Majesty," my Guardian responds, leaving his place behind my chair and stepping into the light. Hearing him being called a 'mindbreaker' makes me feel a little queasy. It sounds far too violent for my gentle, funny Guardian.

"But he's got a block on his mind. Someone's preventing me from breaking through. Someone strong, very strong. Maybe Yer Majesty will be able ta, but nae me."

"Mmhm. Angus doesn't have strong mind powers, but maybe one of his Gods or Guardians does. Someone should find out." She shoots a pointed look at Tamara who smiles and makes a note on her clipboard. Once again, she's sitting in the background, not by the Council table. It doesn't make sense to me, seeing as most of the people in the room will know her real role, but it's probably Tamara's wish to stay in the shadows.

"Ada, try again tomorrow. Theodore, when will he be without pain?"

"I don't know much about dragon physiology," the healer hedges but one stern look by my mother makes him forego the excuses.

"Tomorrow morning, I assume, or the afternoon the latest. His cramps are already lessening, but it may take a while for him to be completely pain-free."

Beira smiles coldly. "We don't need him pain-free, we just need him coherent enough to talk."

"Then early tomorrow morning, my Queen. I will make sure of it."

"Good. Algonquin, any words from the dragon ambassador?"

The librarian shakes his head. "None yet, I will inform you as soon as I hear something, your Majesty."

"If he doesn't soon, we'll have to prepare our own envoy to visit the Dragon Realm. It's not acceptable for one of theirs to come here like one of Angus' spies. I thought the dragons had more honour than that."

"Have you considered that they may have allied with Angus?" Zephyr asks hesitantly, his already wrinkly forehead furrowed.

"Of course," Beira snaps, but her expression softens when she sees the old Guardian shake in fear. Zephyr is used to spending all day with his birds, he's not around people a lot. Storm has told me that the Master of the Wings rarely attends Council meetings unless it's necessary.

"Let's not speculate until we know more. We will reconvene tomorrow at first light. Storm, as I said, at least two of you are to be with Wyn at all times."

Storm bows his head, but then shoots me a grin. He's looking forward to this, but he's going to be disappointed. I need to have a chat with Crispin. Storm's already had his date, but the others haven't. And after what happened between Crisp and me this morning, we need to talk. And maybe kiss.

A girl can hope.

It takes a while for me to persuade Storm and the others to leave me alone with Crispin. Yes, I know my mother said two of them should be with me at all times, but they will be in the room next door. And it's not like Crispin couldn't defend me if necessary. And my magic is the strongest of us all anyway. I have to repeat my arguments several times until they finally leave.

Now I'm alone with Crispin, sitting by yet another fire, and am feeling slightly awkward. How do I start this conversation without it being totally embarrassing?

Luckily, he's a gentleman and does it for me.

"Earlier, did you feel something strange when we... ehm... climaxed?" he asks and I nod enthusiastically.

"Yes, I was going to ask the same. It was like... like we connected? Mentally?"

"Exactly! I felt like I could see inside your mind, just for a moment. It was strange but felt... right, somehow. Like it was meant to be. That doesn't make sense, does it."

"Yes it does. I felt the same. No idea how, but I also got a glimpse into your mind. Although, maybe not your mind. Your memories."

His eyes widen slightly. "What did you see?"

"I'm not quite sure how to describe it. I didn't see pictures, but I felt what you felt in the past. Crispin, I don't know what happened, but I'm so sorry that you had to feel so much pain."

He jumps up. "I don't want to talk about it."

I get up as well and put a hand on his shoulder. It first feels like he's going to shake me off, but he remains there, breathing heavily.

"Have you ever told anyone?" I ask softly.

"No," he whispers. "And I'm not going to. It's the past, it's gone."

"But it's not." I walk around him and give him a gentle hug. He's stiff as a board but I want him to feel that I'm there for him. That I care. "It's why you didn't let me close, right? It's why you almost strangled me when you showed me how your healing magic works, back in Chesca's cottage. It's not gone, it's still here with you, and I think you need to deal with it."

He shoves me away and I stumble backwards.

"You know nothing! You have no clue! Don't tell me to deal

with things you wouldn't understand!" His voice is getting louder and his face reddens.

"You've had it easy all your life! Your mother loved you, loves you still! You were born of love, not created to be a killer, a monster, a..."

Tears are running down his face as he stops shouting. He's looking so lost, so forlorn. Against my better judgement, I walk towards him, my arms wide open, an invitation for him.

"You don't know what I've done," he whispers, his tears freely flowing. I can feel my own tears threatening to come.

"It doesn't matter. You didn't choose to do what you did, right?"

I take another step forwards. "Tell me about it, Crispin. Get it off your chest. Tell me how I can help."

"You can't help me. She made me, destroyed all the good in me, then discarded me in pieces. I'm broken, Wyn, and you won't be able to fix me. It was a mistake to give in, I should have stayed away. I should have stayed strong. You've got the other three, you don't need me..."

That's it. I embrace him, holding him tight.

"I need you," I whisper into his ear, pressing him close as his chest heaves. "I need you and I want you to be mine. Earlier today... it was special. Please don't throw that away. We can work together, we can put the pieces back together. Both of us."

I kiss his cheek. "I need you, Crisp."

His tears are dripping on my shoulders and running down my back. I'm glad he's crying. It means he trusts me enough to do so in front of me. He knows I'd never judge him for it. In contrary, I admire him for showing his feelings. Not many men do nowadays.

"I can't talk about it," he whispers, finally returning my hug. "It's too painful."

I rub his back and notice that his breathing is becoming slower. Good.

"Can you write it down? Or tell somebody else? Paint it? You need to get it off your chest somehow. Sharing it will help."

"How do you know that?"

"Growing up without my mother wasn't easy. I knew from the beginning that I was adopted, my parents never hid that fact. When Beira visited me, she was cold and distant. Then she left and wouldn't contact me for a long time. I felt abandoned, lonely, unwanted. In my teens, I became depressed."

I pause and this time, it's he who's rubbing my back to reassure me. I've not told many people what I'm telling him now.

"I didn't even know it was depression. It wasn't that I was sad all the time or crying. No, I was feeling... empty, wrong, and emotionless. I couldn't laugh about jokes anymore. I became withdrawn. I didn't have the energy to meet friends or go out after school. I became a bit of a hermit, rarely leaving my room. Luckily, my parents noticed something was wrong and made me see a therapist. It took a while for me to open up, but talking helped. Of course I couldn't mention that Beira is a Goddess and living in another Realm, so I told her that my mother was living abroad. By talking about it, I realised how abandoned I really felt. And once I knew what was wrong, I could deal with it."

"I'm sorry you had to go through that," Crispin says slowly. "Did Beira tell you why she had to give you up?"

"Yes, and it explained a lot. But enough about me. I've dealt with my demons. I think it's time for you to deal with yours."

"I really don't think I can talk about it. But I may be able to show you, if Arc helps us. But that would mean that you'll have to see it. I wouldn't want to do that to anyone."

I step back and smile at him. I want him to see that I'm meaning what I'm about to say.

"I'll do it. For you. For us. We'll get through this, Crisp, together."

I kiss him for emphasis.

"Aye, I can do it. I dinnae have ta be with ya, either, but if ya want ta stop it, I need ta be there."

We've asked Arc to join us in my chambers and it looks like he'll be able to link our minds so I can see Crispin's memories. I'm a bit scared now, but I can't let my blond Guardian know that. He's still struggling with the idea of showing me what happened to him in the past. It must have been something terrible.

Back at Chesca's cottage, after he almost strangled me, the others told me a bit about his past. How he was created by the Morrigan to be her torturer. How she forced him to corrupt his healing magic into something that would bring pain and death to the Goddess's foes. And how she created a sister for him to keep him under control. A sister who died, somehow, when Beira took Crispin away from the Morrigan.

I steel myself for what I'm about to see. Knowing a bit helps me to prepare, but the guys also told me that all they know is hearsay, not something that Crispin told them. So maybe nothing of it is true.

I guess I'll find out.

"I'd prefer if it's just Wyn and me," Crispin says quietly. "But I'd understand if you'd be able to stop it, Princess."

"No, you lived it, so I should be able to watch it," I say with determination. "Let's do this."

"It's best if ya lie doon on the bed. And I'll get the others ta keep watch, all three of us will be busy."

We do as he says, lying next to each other, holding hands. Arc gets the others, then sits down on a chair by the bed.

"Is this safe?" Storm asks sceptically, but I ignore him. It's important, that's what it is. Who cares about safe. And I mean what I said: if Crispin lived through it, I should be ashamed if I can't look at his memories.

"I'm ready."

Crispin squeezes my hand.

"I'm not, but let's do this."

"Okay. Crisp, ya need ta start with something simple. A good memory. That will help bind ya two together. Then go back and show her what ya need. If ya want ta stop, ya need ta think of the present. Wyn, ya won't be able to influence anything. Crisp is the driver, yer the passenger."

I smile. "I trust him."

"Good. Close yer eyes. Wyn, think of Crisp. Crisp, think of Wyn. Think of yer bond."

I do as he says, thinking back to earlier, when Crispin was inside me, holding me tight. I smile at the memory.

Then my own memory dissolves and something else takes its place.

Darkness.

Chapter Ten

I open my eyes and look into my own. A grey, slightly misty Wyn is smiling at me. No, not at me, at the dream-Crispin standing just behind me. I step out of the way, letting the two look at each other.

"Where are we?" I ask the very real Crispin next to me. In stark contrast to his dream self, he's solid and in full colour. The world around us is like an echo, depicting the world but not quite in the same way.

"Take a guess."

I look around. We're just outside my mother's Palace, on a path leading to one of the villages. There are five of them, circling the Palace grounds, home to some of the staff and other Guardians wanting to live close to the Queen. Now I remember. Crispin took me to see one of them, Baton Town (definitely not a town, don't ask me why they would call a village with maybe a hundred houses that), and to visit a friend of his. Somehow, I'd never considered that my Guardians may have friends outside their close-knit group.

The friend turned out to be Lucas, a broad, wild man who was the village's smith. He certainly looked like he could swing a hammer. He was nice, but far too obsessed by me being the Princess. He mainly talked to Crispin, ignoring me. Luckily my Guardian noticed how uncomfortable both Lucas and I were, so we left pretty soon after we arrived.

On the way back, we'd stopped, which I think is where we are now. I didn't want to go back to the confined walls of the Palace and all the rules I had to follow.

"We could go for a quick flight," dream-Crispin says.

The real Crispin puts a hand on my shoulder and points at dream-Wyn.

"Look at your eyes light up at my words. Look how you smile. You're radiant. You were so happy, so beautiful. It made me realise how important little things are... how even flying for a few minutes could make you happy. And how you being happy makes me feel good."

I turn around and spontaneously kiss Crispin. He's surprised, but it doesn't take him long to respond. His lips are soft on mine, his kiss gentle. I love how all of my Guardians have their own unique way of kissing. And none of them is better than the other; they're all just right.

When we break apart, his smile is turning sad.

"I think it's time to go back to the beginning. Please remember, the Crispin you will see is not who I am now. He was raw... hurting. Manipulated. He was born to be evil, and it took him a while to see that it was wrong." He sighs. "I'm not sure this is a good idea. I don't want you to think bad of me."

I take his hand and give it a reassuring squeeze.

"Don't worry. Whatever you're going to show me, it's not going to change how I think of you. You're my Crispy."

I laugh and he joins me.

"Please don't ever call me that again. Once was enough. I'm still angry at Blaze for giving you his sparklies."

"Yeah, me too. But I like Crispy. It's cute."

He growls. "I'm not cute."

"Yes, you are. My cute Guardian who I'd love to kiss and cuddle right now." I sigh. "But let's be responsible and get this over with."

He nods, but it's clear how reluctant he is. He's only doing this to make me happy. Although I'm not sure 'happy' is the right word. By wanting to please me, I hope he's going to be able to deal with his demons.

In a flash, the scenery changes. We're in a dark room that could be anywhere. The walls are stone, illuminated only by a small ball of light hovering by the ceiling. It's not enough light to see properly, but something is moving in one corner. I walk towards it, curious. There's a shape... a man. He's sitting propped up against the wall, as if he's exhausted, but when I get closer, I can see that he's got a collar around the neck. He's shackled against the wall and is struggling to move into a more comfortable position.

Another step forwards... and my eyes see what my heart already knew. It's Crispin. His blond hair is dirty and tousled, the clothes he's wearing are no more than rags. He's looking thin and frail, so unlike the Guardian standing behind me now.

My heart breaks for dream-Crispin, and it breaks again when I remember that this was real, once upon a time. This isn't a dream, this is a memory.

"I'd been created about a month earlier," the real Crispin whispers as if not to disturb the memory. "When I opened my eyes for the first time, the most beautiful woman was smiling at me. I didn't know what was happening, but I felt at home. With that woman in my life, everything just had to be good. I smiled back at her. Then she hit me. Again and again. I didn't know what was happening, what I'd done. I tried to defend myself, but it was as if my arms were glued to my sides. She punched me in the stomach, slapped my face, even kneed me between the legs. When she stopped, all I felt was pain. She released the spell on me and I fell to the ground, too weak to stand. She kneeled by my side and smiled again, the same smile she'd given me when I first woke. 'I'm going to enjoy you,' she said, and left. It became a daily ritual. She'd come, smile at me and beat me. I lost consciousness a few times. But because of my healing magic, I would be healthy again by the next time she came. My life became pain, nothing but pain."

He points at dream-Crispin. "I tried to escape. This was the day after. She dragged me to this room, put a collar around my neck and shackled me to the wall. Because of the position of the collar, I had to sit in a half-bent position. It was agony. She'd managed to keep me in pain even while she wasn't with me."

The door opens, interrupting him. I'm almost glad for the break. It's unbearable to see him in pain, to hear what he had to go through. But on the other hand, I'm impressed that he's actually telling me about it.

A woman enters. That must be *her*. His creator. The Morrigan.

She's stunning. Sleek black hair falls to her waist, matching her charcoal eyes. Her skin is pale but radiant, the kind of ivory, flawless skin most women would kill for. Her high cheekbones give her a haughty look and her slightly curled lips only add to her majesty. She's looking as much as a Queen as Beira does. But while Beira has a cold, detached air, the Morrigan exudes cruelty. She doesn't reign with wisdom. She does it by force and punishment.

"My little boy, how are you feeling?" She goes on her knees in front of dream-Crispin and draws a pale finger along his jaw, forcing him to look at her.

He doesn't respond, and I'm proud of him for showing this defiance despite being so weak.

"I'm so glad you tried to escape. I thought I'd have to continue the beatings for even longer," she says sweetly and he looks at her in confusion.

"Oh yes, you were supposed to escape. It's the sign that you are ready for the next stage of your training."

She snaps her fingers and Crispin's collar falls off, releasing him. He crumples to the floor, stretching his back. He must be in agony after being in the same uncomfortable position for so long.

The Morrigan smiles at him, but her eyes remain cruel.

"I'm sorry I had to do this to you. It didn't give me any pleasure. But you needed to understand pain. How could you give pain without first having felt it?"

That bitch. I want to kill her, right here, right now, but of course that isn't possible. This is a memory, not reality.

Dream-Crispin is suddenly lifted from the floor until he's floating upright.

"Come with me, darling," the Morrigan says, as if he has a choice. She leaves the room and he floats behind her, his expression making it obvious that he's struggling against the hold she has on him. But of course, as one of the main Goddesses, she has a lot more power than any Guardian could ever hope to have.

I turn to the real Crispin. Tears are running down his face.

"I don't think I can do this," he whispers. "I don't want to see what she did next. What I did."

I embrace him, putting as much warmth and love as I can into the hug. He's hurting and I don't want to see him in pain, but I also know it's necessary. He needs to show me what happened. Even though I'm scared to find out what she did to him. She's now number one on my to-kill list, even above Angus. If I ever meet her in person, it will end in bloodshed.

"Let's do this together. You can do this. I'm so proud of you already." I kiss him on the cheek. "Crispy."

Despite his tears, he chuckles.

"I told you not to call me that."

"What are you going to do to stop me?" I tease, hoping that he will play along.

But he never gets the chance. A scream tears through the quiet and Crispin's eyes widen. It wasn't his voice. Someone else is screaming, another man.

I take my Guardian's hand and pull him with me, out of the room and along the corridor where the Morrigan walked not too long ago. When we come to a crossing, I look at Crispin, not knowing in which direction to turn. The screams have stopped so we can't follow them.

He sighs heavily and turns right, leading the way. We enter a large room, brightly lit. In the middle is a metal table and on it lies a man, naked, his wrists and ankles chained. The Morrigan is standing at the end of the table, smiling down on the man in front of her. Is she ever not smiling?

Dream-Crispin is standing by her side, no longer hovering but looking as if he's barely keeping himself upright. He's definitely too weak to run and the Goddess knows that. He's staring at the man with a strange expression. Is it... hate?

"Do you recognise him, my darling?" the Morrigan asks dream-Crispin in her high-pitched voice.

"He beat me," he whispers hoarsely and she nods with an indulgent smile.

"Yes, my dear, he beat you. What a terrible man. But now you can return the favour. You see, he did some bad things and I need to punish him. Will you help me?"

She's talking to Crispin as if he's a child. Her fake smile is aggravating me and I want to wipe it off her perfect face. If only this was real.

"It's really easy. Push your magic into him until you feel his body like your own."

She puts an arm around dream-Crispin and leads him to the naked man's side. My Guardian is wide-eyed, but he doesn't resist her as she puts his right hand on the man's stomach. The prisoner begins to struggle even more.

"Close your eyes," the Morrigan chirps and dream-Crispin does as she says.

"Now push your magic into his body, not his mind."

I shudder as I remember Crispin teaching me just that back at Chesca's cottage. That was just before he almost strangled me. No wonder it was such a trigger for him.

"Very good, my dear," she whispers sweetly. "Now search for the nerves in his back."

Dream-Crispin nods as if he's in a trance. He's under her spell, even if he doesn't know it.

"Now make him feel pain. Remember how he beat you. Make him feel the same agony. Stimulate the nerves until he can't take it any longer."

The naked man begins to scream again. It's a high-pitched wail that's tearing at my heartstrings. I want to help him, but there's no way I can. Dream-Crispin's forehead is furrowed in concentration, but he doesn't stop whatever he's doing. The prisoner's legs are twitching uncontrollably and his screams are getting louder.

A sob makes me look at the real Crispin next to me. His face is pale, his eyes bloodshot.

"I wasn't myself," he whispers. "I wasn't myself. I wasn't myself."

"Shhh, it will be okay." I try to comfort him, but he avoids my eyes, evading my touch.

"Of course you weren't yourself. The Crispin I know would never hurt anyone," I reassure him, but the screams of the man in front of us tell a different story. Goosebumps are covering my skin as I see a smile on dream-Crispin's face. Please don't... I don't want to see him like that. Better to see him chained up in that dark room than seeing him smile while torturing a man.

The Morrigan is laughing, patting dream-Crispin's head like a dog.

"You're even better than I imagined! Oh darling, I'm so proud of you!"

The real Crispin sinks on his knees, hugging himself. I kneel next to him, extending an arm to hug him, but he shakes his head.

"Don't."

Turning away and getting up is one of the hardest things I've ever done. He's hurting and I can't bear seeing him like that. But I also want to respect his wishes. I need to give him space.

Wiping away a tear, I look back at the memory in front of me. The man on the table is no longer moving, but his chest is moving up and down, so at least he's not dead. Dream-Crispin has opened his eyes and is now looking at the Morrigan with a dreamy expression. What's happening? Has he forgotten what she did to him? How she beat him every day for a month? How she chained him to a wall like an animal?

"Tomorrow, you can do the same thing again. Would you like that? Hurting the man who hurt you?"

Her voice is sweet, but I can hear the venom in it. She is poisoning Crispin's mind and she's succeeding. He's vulnerable, knowing nothing but abuse. I have to remember that he's only a month old at this point. She's being nice to him and he's greedily latching on to that. Would I act any different?

Without warning, the scene changes. We're in a dark hallway, the only light is coming from the moon outside the tall windows. In front of us, dream-Crispin is sneaking down the corridor, keeping close to the wall, hiding in the shadows. I check on the real Crispin next to me. His face is a mask of fear, but he gives me a brave nod.

"You're doing so well," I reassure him. "Don't forget how strong you are. Just being here proves that."

He smiles a little and I turn back to dream-Crispin, my heart feeling a little lighter. No matter how small his smile was, it gives me hope that he'll get through this.

We follow the ghostly shape through a maze of corridors until we reach an ornate door. Dream-Crispin opens it soundlessly and we hurry to follow him before he closes the door again.

It's a bedroom, richly decorated with tapestries and expensive carpets. In the middle of the room is a four-poster bed. This is the home of someone rich, no doubt about that.

Dream-Crispin tiptoes to the bed, looking down at the person sleeping in it. He reaches out and touches the woman's chest. She's old, her white hair is spread around her head on the pillow. He closes his eyes and the woman stops breathing.

He killed her.

Crispin assassinated someone.

Oh Gods. So it's true. Crispin was a killer.

Without a look back at the dead woman, dream-Crispin leaves the room. We follow him until he's outside the house. He expands his wings and jumps into the air.

I give the real Crispin a questioning look and he nods.

"We need to follow him. I'll explain in the air."

I spread my wings and fly. The exhilarating feeling I usually get when flying doesn't come. I'm too busy trying to avoid thinking of the dead woman in her four-poster bed. Who was she? What did she do to have to die?

We fly silently, following dream-Crispin through the night. He's fast as if he has to get to his destination in a hurry.

"At this point, I had been her assassin for decades," Crispin begins quietly and I have to strain to hear him. "I killed and tortured whenever she commanded. It became my life. She'd tell me what to do and I did it. Then she'd smile at me and for a moment, a ray of sunshine came into the darkness inside me. I lived for her smiles. I wanted her to be proud of me.

"She was the only person I ever spoke to. She took care to keep me isolated. I never spoke to my victims. I gave them pain or death, but I never talked to them. I slept in a room connected to hers, and sometimes she would come to mine at night to tell me how good I was being. Then I smiled and slept well, thinking of how happy I made her. I'd forgotten all about the pain she'd made me suffer at the beginning.

"I don't remember everything of that time. I was a shell, doing what I was told, not thinking about what it meant to kill someone. I existed but I didn't live.

"But over time, things slowly changed. I guess I developed a conscience. It began slowly. I would use less painful methods to torture her victims. I wouldn't prolong death like she sometimes commanded. I'd claim I'd lost control of my magic, but she soon noticed that I was no longer as loyal as I had been. So she came up with a new way to control me. Lily."

Chapter Eleven

Dawn is rising. A golden sheen spans the horizon, matching the note of hope in Crispin's tale.

Dream-Crispin is descending and we follow him. We're approaching a dark palace, almost as big as my mother's, but instead of white stone, it's all black. The turrets are jagged and spiky, seemingly piercing the sky. It's not a welcoming place, but it looks like it's our destination.

Dream-Crispin lands on one of the towers and a moment later, we do the same. We descend along a narrow staircase until we reach a simple circular room. It doesn't have any doors besides one leading to a small bathroom; the only way to reach it is from the roof. Not a problem for Guardians, though, and I assume that the Morrigan has wings as well.

The only furniture in the room is a bed, a wardrobe and a crib. Dream-Crispin hurries to the latter and picks up a baby from it.

Oh. Lily. Is that the sister Storm mentioned when he told me about Crispin's past?

She's sleeping, happily suckling on her thumb. Dream-Crispin is smiling widely as he carries her over to the bed and sits down with her in his arms. His eyes are full of love for the little baby. He looks a lot more like the Crispin I know. Warm, happy, gentle. Not at all like the Crispin we saw not long ago, killing a defenceless woman. I feel queasy. It doesn't go together in my head how this can be one and the same person. The ruthless killer and the man smiling at a baby.

The real Crispin walks to the bed and looks down at the sleeping girl. A tear runs down his face, but he's smiling. A sad smile, but it's a smile nonetheless.

"She was an experiment," he begins, never turning his gaze away from the baby. "The Mistress... the Morrigan wanted to see if a Guardian created in the shape of a baby would grow. When she didn't, I was told to kill her. But I couldn't. Even in my dark state of mind, I couldn't kill a baby. When I refused, the Morrigan smiled. Before, I would have done anything for that smile, but suddenly, I found it revolting. Lily opened my eyes to the Morrigan's cruelty, but she used that against me. I was given Lily to care for, something I did gladly. But in return for Lily's safety, I had to do what was demanded of me. I had to become the cruel monster again that I had just started to leave behind."

Dream-Crispin is gently stroking the fluffy hair on Lily's head. It's strange to think that she'll be a baby for all her life. How cruel of the Morrigan to even do an experiment like that. But then, after what I've seen today, it shouldn't surprise me. Life means nothing to her, all she wants is pain and destruction. She seems to thrive off it. And to think that Crispin was her slave for so long... My heart is too broken to break again. It's going to take me a while to get my head around it all. How my beautiful, amazing Crispin started off as a heartless murderer, doing the Morrigan's every wish... no. I can't understand how that happened.

"Around that time, I learned that I was a wanted man," Crispin resumes his tale. "They thought I was a lone assassin, they didn't know about the Morrigan having me under her control. It was Beira herself who commanded that I had to be caught. So I made a plan. The Morrigan was threatening Lily more with every day, but I couldn't continue killing on her behalf. I needed to find a way out."

The scene changes, with the room turning into a very familiar place. My mother's bedchamber.

I shoot Crispin a questioning look but he doesn't respond, instead looking at dream-Crispin who is sneaking towards my mother's bed. It reminds me of the scene we watched earlier, where he assassinated the old woman. Surely, he's not going to try and kill Beira?

No. When he reaches her bedside, he kneels on the floor, bowing his head.

"Your Majesty," he says loud and clear and Beira sits up, wide awake.

"I was wondering what you were going to do. So you're the famous assassin?"

If he's surprised that she knew he was in the room, he doesn't let on.

"I'm here to hand myself in. I only ask that you will free someone from the claws of the Goddess who has held me captive."

"And who may that be?" my mother asks coldly.

"The Morrigan."

A look of shock passes over my mother's face before her usual mask returns.

"You say the Morrigan has held you captive?"

Dream-Crispin nods. "She created me and forced me to do her bidding. I killed on her command, but that is no excuse. Do with me what you want, but please free Lily. She's another one of the Morrigan's creations, but she's innocent. She needs to be saved, she doesn't deserve to die."

"And why would I do that and interfere with the business of another Goddess?"

I can't believe my mother just said that. Surely, she's responsible for the deeds of the other Gods? She's the highest of them all, with the exception of Angus, of course.

"Because you're the Mother of Gods," Dream-Crispin says quietly. "You wouldn't let anyone suffer who you could help."

"Wouldn't I?" My mother's voice is as cold as ever, but there's a slight smile on her lips.

"No, you wouldn't." Crispin's conviction is clear and I'm sure my mother sees that as well.

She sighs. "You will have to tell me more about what the Morrigan has been doing."

I turn away as he begins his sorry tale, holding on to the real Crispin. We cry together as dream-Crispin speaks of all the pain he brought in the Morrigan's name. How she killed hundreds, if not thousands of people. How she experimented on Guardians, how she created abominations only to torture and kill them shortly after. It's worse than I could have imagined.

"How did you survive?" I whisper.

"I don't know. I guess I didn't live until I met Lily."

"What happened to her?"

He clings to me as he takes a deep breath.

"The Morrigan killed her when Beira stormed her palace. And then she escaped. It was all for nothing. Lily died and the Morrigan disappeared. The life I had just began to live disappeared in front of my eyes. I wanted to die, I didn't feel like I deserved to live. But Beira didn't let me. She didn't even imprison me for what I'd done. Instead, she sent me to live with Freya, one of her friends.

"Freya didn't know who I was. She thought Beira had sent me to her as a present, as a new lover. I wasn't her type, but she kept me anyway. Taught me how to play chess, how to drink, how to laugh. She helped me forget. We should visit her sometime."

We break apart. His tears have dried and so have mine. I'm seething inside that the Morrigan escaped justice, but I am happy that in the end, Crispin managed to start a new life. But I tear up again when I think of Lily. How can you kill a baby? There's nothing more innocent than a new-born child. Rage is filling my veins. The Morrigan was never punished, but somehow, I will make sure that she will be. She needs to pay for what she did. And I will make sure she does, even if it's the last thing I do.

We wake up in each other's arms. Crispin is looking at me hesitantly, as if he's not sure if I've changed my mind about him.

In response, I kiss him on the nose.

Arc chuckles from behind me.

"Shall I join ya?"

"No, Crispin and I need some alone time," I say resolutely and with a disappointed snort, Arc leaves and takes the other two Guardians with him.

"Are you okay?" I gently ask Crispin. He hesitates before answering.

"I'm not sure. I think I need to get used to the idea that someone... you... saw my memories. I've never told anyone and now... I'm not sure what to think."

"Take your time, but I'm always there to talk."

"I know." He smiles. "You were right. Sharing did make me feel better. Thank you."

"Anytime," I whisper. "How about some distraction?"

He frowns. "You still want me? After seeing all that?"

I move closer to him until our bodies touch. "Yes. I'll always want you."

And to drive the point home, I slide my hands under his shirt, touching his smooth chest.

With one sudden move, he pulls me on top of himself until I'm straddling him. His mouth seeks mine and he kisses me hungrily. I return the kiss, nudging his tongue with mine, showing him that I want him. All of him. His past, his present, his future.

I 'm thankful to the others for giving us some alone time. Well, almost an entire alone day. They probably think we've been at it like rabbits, but we didn't actually do anything more than kiss. Maybe a bit of touching, too, but I think neither of us had the energy for more. So we just lay there, holding each other, giving each other comfort. Just because I've seen Crispin's wounds doesn't mean that they've automatically healed. On the contrary, I think he's raw right now, with old memories returning to the surface. He woke me a few times, whimpering in his sleep. I feel bad for putting him through this, but I also know that it's necessary. He's no use to anyone if he can't step away from his past.

I watch him as he sleeps: his messy blond hair is covering his forehead, his mouth is relaxed with a hint of a smile, despite everything he's been through. Even though I saw some of his past, I know that he only showed me a few select glimpses. There must have been more terrible things that happened to him, but you wouldn't know it looking at him. He has no scars on his skin, but they linger just below it, hidden from view until you look beneath the surface. I'm glad I did. It makes me love him even more. And understand why he held back for so long.

I'm not sure how yet, but I'm going to make the Morrigan pay for this. I need to talk to my mother, maybe she knows where the Goddess is hiding. There must be rumours; a Goddess as pompous and proud as the Morrigan can't just disappear without leaving a trace. Does my mother keep tabs on all the Gods she created?

I hope she does.

"Good morning," Crispin whispers sleepily and I swipe my thoughts away. Those can wait.

"How did you sleep?"

"Is it cheesy to say that I slept well knowing you were sleeping next to me?"

I chuckle. "Yes, I'd call that cheesy. But it's okay to be like that occasionally." I don't mention that I'm aware of all his tossing and turning, of his whimpers. He obviously didn't sleep well, but I'm going to let that pass for now.

"You look cute when your hair is all frazzled," he mumbles, still not quite awake.

I laugh and ruffle his hair.

"You're kind of cute as well. Do you want to sleep a bit longer?"

He looks tempted but he shakes his head. "I think we have some work to do. Let's find out if your mother has any news for us about the assassin they caught. They should have been able to interrogate him by now."

My heart sinks at the thought. I've not been here long enough to know what kind of interrogating they do in the Realm. Is it medieval torture? Or mind magic like Arc can do? Or simply questioning without violence? It's hard to tell - some things here are quite old-fashioned, but at the same time, my mother is a lot less violent than people think. She's actually got a good heart, no matter how thick the icy shell around it is.

The assassin doesn't look very evil. More like a sad Viking with a mop of dirty blond hair, a broad stature and shabby clothes.

He's sitting in his cell, hugging his legs, looking quite lost. He's young, maybe in his mid-twenties. He doesn't look like a dragon either, but then, I've never met one of them before. I assume they're like the werewolves people tell stories about on Earth who can shift between shapes. If not, then it's a very disappointing dragon.

The cell isn't like I imagined it either. It's not a dark dungeon with iron bars. Instead, it's a white room with no bars or door at all. A shimmering, translucent wall of thin ice is all that's between him and us. It looks brittle, but I'm sure it's as strong as crystal. The only prisoner to have ever escaped my mother's Palace was Colan, my father, and I'm not sure if she maybe let him escape.

Ada and her Guardians are standing guard, watching the prisoner carefully. They bow to me as I turn away from the assassin.

"Has he talked yet?"

Ada grimaces. "Yes, but nothing that would help us. He's babbling about mates and bonds, but none of it makes sense. I think he might not be quite right in the head."

The man perks up when he hears Ada's voice. Apparently, the barrier between us and his cell is not soundproof.

"Don't resist the mating call," he suddenly shouts, his eyes crazed as he stares at Ada, before sinking back into his previous position.

"See what I mean?" Ada sighs in frustration. "Nothing we've tried so far has worked. The healer says he's okay physically, but clearly his mind isn't. If only we knew if he's always like that or if it's caused by something." She lowers his voice. "I almost feel sorry for him."

To be honest, so do I. I know he tried to kill me, but right now, he looks like a broken man, rocking back and forth as if he's in pain. He's nothing like the dark figure I remember seeing in my room before I passed out. If they're one and the same, he's changed a lot.

"Did the poison have a lasting effect on him?" I ask, thinking that may be the cause of his deterioration.

"Theodore says no. But then, it's not the first time he's been wrong."

When she sees my questioning glance, she blushes. "I probably shouldn't tell you this..."

I sigh. "Out with it, Ada."

"He predicted that you would die as soon as you were born. He didn't believe that the child of Beira and a simple Guardian would be able to survive."

I laugh. "Well, I proved him wrong in that regard."

She smiles in relief. She probably expected a different response from me, but it's not like I see the healer as infallible. When my magic was locked, he didn't find a cure for that. And when my mother was almost killed by the Summer King's assassin, it was me who saved her, not him. I wonder why Crispin isn't the Royal Physician, I'm sure he's a lot more skilled than Theodore. But then I think of Crispin's trauma and know why. He's not reliable. But he will be. Now that he's started fighting his inner demons, everything will get better for him. I hope.

"What's the next step with him?" I ask Ada, pointing at the prisoner.

"Her Majesty is going to talk to him later today. Maybe she will be able to get something out of him. Arc tried and failed - which means this guy is either completely crazed or has some very strong mental barriers. I bet on the former - I mean, look at him. Does he look very strong to you?"

She blushes slightly. "I mean mentally. Physically, he's quite strong."

Ada is doing a lot of blushing today. That's not like her. Her three Guardians seems to have noticed that as well. One of them – I can never keep them apart - is glaring at the prisoner as if he's competition. I'm glad my guys aren't as jealous... or if they are, they're not as obvious about it.

"Princess?"

A maid comes running down the corridor.

"Yes?"

"You're late for the dress fitting, ma'am." She's completely out of breath. She must take dress fittings seriously.

"I didn't know I had one."

"It's for the ball tonight, your Highness."

"I didn't know about that one either."

The girl looks as if she's about to faint.

Ada winks at me. "You better go before the seamstress herself comes looking for you. I hear she's quite formidable."

On days like these I wish I was just a simple Guardian like Ada. Not that she's simple, she's the deputy Master of Arms after all, but for festivities all she has to do is put on her dress uniform. She doesn't have to worry about dresses and itchy fabrics and chest-squeezing corsets.

Chapter Twelve

Two hours of being prodded, measured and tortured, the seamstress finally shuffles off, leaving me alone with four rather amused Guardians.

"I'm still amazed how you let yourself be treated like that," Frost observes with a wide grin. "If she'd come close to me with those giant needles, I'd have thrown her to the other side of the room."

I grimace. "I don't think it would make a good impression if the heiress to the throne started throwing people around. People might actually tell my mother." I shiver. As nice as Beira is to me in private, as cold she is in public. I've tried to stay in her good books and so far, it's worked. Mostly. In fact, she approved of Arc and my plans to contact my parents.

Tomorrow's the day. Today, I will have to endure yet another ball, thrown in the honour of some random God. My mother is pulling all the stops to get the other Gods on her side, and if that means throwing one ball after the next, so be it. I've not met many Gods yet, in fact, only one, I think. And he was a complete disappointment.

We covered the Egyptian God Ra back at school and I always imagined him as a radiant, imposing figure. Nope, he definitely wasn't imposing. He was a shy hunchback with a surprised expression whenever he was addressed, as if he wasn't used to being talked to. I gave up pretty quickly and let my mother deal with him.

But tonight, rumour has it – aka the seamstress told me – that Loki might be among the guests. I wonder if he looks anything like he does in the films. And maybe his brother, Thor, will be there as well... Now that would make attending the ball worth it.

"Who of us are ye thinking of?"

I stare at Arc in confusion.

"Ye've got that swooning look. Like ye want to nibble on one of us."

I blush. I hope they'll never find out that I was thinking about Thor and Loki. Not that I'd ever do something with them... but just because I have four amazing Guardians by my side doesn't mean that I can't appreciate the rest of the male population from afar.

"You, of course," I tease him and give him a quick peck on the cheek. "I was wondering what you're hiding beneath your kilt."

He's wearing one of those again today, a dark green one. Arc lifts it suggestively.

"I could show ya. Or ya could go on yer knees and take a peek."

I laugh. "I wish, but I think there's a Council meeting that we're already running late to."

Arc sighs. "Aye, I ken but I thought I could distract ya."

"It almost worked. But let's pretend to be responsible and not keep Beira waiting."

"We can always blame that monster of a seamstress," Frost suggests. "If she could, she would have kept you here for ages to use you as her personal pin cushion."

Yeah, that's what it felt like. I'm pretty sure she drew blood with some of her needles. Let's hope tonight's dress won't be too uncomfortable and extravagant. I'd be totally happy with a simple dress, but that's wishful thinking.

M ost of the Council is already in attendance by the time we make it into the brightly lit chamber. Some of them are already wearing suits and dresses in preparation for the festivities. Poor Algonquin is looking just as uncomfortable in his suit as I usually am in my ball gowns.

The only ones missing are Theodore and Zephyr.

"Let's begin," my mother announces as soon as we're seated. Our Master of the Wings had an unfortunate accident, but Theodore is tending to him now."

She snaps her fingers and a map appears in the middle of the large table, showing the entire Winter Realm. It's so big that the Royal Palace is only a small dot close to the Northern border. The Gates are marked by glowing red symbols, while the villages and towns are shimmering blue dots.

"We've had reports of Summer spies being sighted here, here and here."

Golden flames flicker into existence on the map. The pattern is clear: they've been spotted close to the Gates.

"If Angus is going to try and attack one of our Gates again like he's done in the past, he's going to be sorely disappointed. Master Gwain has increased the border guards tenfold and the Gates are better protected than they ever have. He won't be able to enter the Realm that way. But it leaves the question how he managed to get the Summer soldiers into my domain. We never found out how he did it last time, but Colan heard two of them mention a mage."

My heart beats faster at the mention of my father. He was mortally wounded by Summer soldiers when they attacked one of the Gates.

"I stand by my opinion that no mage should be able to transport someone from one Realm to another without the use of the Gates," Gwain says in his deep voice. "He must have misheard or the Summer soldiers were aware of him listening and fed him some wrong information."

"Or they believed that it was a mage when in fact it was not." Storm surprises me by speaking up. Usually he's quiet in these meetings. "It can't have been Angus himself, he can't breach the Winter Realm just like our Queen wouldn't be able to enter the Summer Realm. Correct me if I'm wrong."

"You're quite right," Beira says with a smile. "After the last war, we put that precaution in place. Only other Gods would be able to accomplish such a feat, but none of the Gods allied with Angus are strong enough. Unless he has new allies that I don't know about."

It's strange to hear my mother say that she doesn't know something. In my mind, she's almost omniscient, aware of everything that happens in her Realm and beyond. Her not being able to solve this mystery scares me a little.

"How many Gods would be strong enough?" I ask, feeling a little stupid that I don't know them all by heart.

"Seven, maybe eight," Gwain replies. "But none of them are on Angus' side."

"For now, we have to keep the Gates secure and increase the patrols. Spread the message that any Summer spy captures must not be killed but sent here for questioning."

Gwain bows his head. "I'm sorry, your Majesty. My officers have been rebuked for not searching them better when they caught them."

"What happened?" Magnus, the treasurer, asks and I'm grateful that he does. It saves me from having to show my ignorance.

"They took poison while they were being transported to the capital," Gwain explains.

"That seems to become quite a trend. It was the same with the dragon assassin. Has anyone been able to find out if it was the same kind of poison?"

"Sadly, Theodore wasn't able to tell. The symptoms were similar though."

"Which brings us to the prisoner." My mother turns to Ada. "Has there been any progress in getting him to talk?"

"None, your Majesty. He seems out of it most of the time, and when he's lucid, all he talks about are mating bonds and that they brought him to the Palace. It's as if he doesn't know why he did it or can't remember it. Threats have absolutely no effect, nor have punishments. I'm at my wit's end, to be honest."

"I will pay him a visit before the ball," Beira promises. She's told me in confidence that she's worried the raw power of her mind might kill him. And together with her anger that he managed to assassinate me, the chances are that he might not survive an encounter with the Winter Queen. That's why so far, she's let others deal with the interrogation, but it looks like she no longer has a choice. They've been getting nowhere. It's time for Beira to meet the strange dragon assassin.

"I was hoping that Zephyr might be able to tell us if the Dragon Ambassador has replied yet, but that will have to wait until he's healed. Algonquin, have you found out more about the poison?"

"Yes, your Majesty," the librarian responds in his quiet, raspy voice. I pity him whenever he has to speak up. He's got the air of someone who would rather spend his time with books than people.

"It's a plant that's not native to either the Dragon Realm nor the Winter Realm."

"The Summer Realm, then?" Gwain asks. "It would make sense that they're working with Angus."

"I'm afraid it's more complicated than that. As far as I'm aware, it can only be found in the Demon Realm."

There are gasps across the room.

"But the demons are not allied with anyone." Ada frowns, vocalising what's on everybody's mind. "They have never shown any interest in the Gods or us Guardians. The only dealing we have with them is preventing them from doing too many raids on the humans."

I wonder if Chesca would have a different opinion on that. From what she said, some Guardians saw it as a rite of passage to travel to the Demon Realm and kill as many demons as possible. Aodh had been different from those Guardians though, trying to bring demons to change their ways. He'd only killed them if he didn't have a choice. Some demons loved travelling to Earth to kill humans, and Guardians were responsible for bringing them to justice. Ada made it sound clinical; 'preventing' was just a fancy word for killing.

But my Guardians and I are probably the only people in this room who had actually talked to a demon. And eaten her food. I shudder as I think back to the disgusting scones she had served me. I wonder where she is now. Still on Earth in their little cottage? Or back among her own kind, now that she no longer has Aodh to keep her in check.

"That complicates things. And you're sure that plant doesn't grow anywhere else?" my mother asks Algonquin, who looks like he wants to be anywhere but in this room.

"If it does, it's not mentioned in any book on herbology we have in the Royal Library. I've gone through them all with the help of my assistants, and the two times we found it described in detail, it was always in relation to the Demon Realm."

"Could someone simply have imported it from there?" Ada asks, once again speaking what's on my mind. She's young for a Guardian and the least experienced in this room.

"Nobody trades with demons," Gwain responds with disdain. "And I can't imagine anyone travelling there just to pluck a herb. There are other effective poisons out there; it doesn't make sense for anyone to go through all that trouble unless they actually lived there."

"It's rather curious that Wyn was given black dragon venom and not this demon plant," my mother whispers almost to herself.

A bell rings through the Palace, the sign that visitors have started to arrive.

Beira sighs. "Let's reconvene tomorrow. Tamara, please tell the Lord Chamberlain to look after my guests while I go and see the prisoner."

She gets up from her throne-like chair and everybody follows suit. She sweeps out of the room, her dress transforming from simple blue silk into something a lot more regal. I wish I could do that. Instead, I will have to go back to my quarters and get dressed the normal way. Hopefully with just my maids, not that terrible seamstress.

My Guardians are looking splendid in their suits... well, all except for Arc. He's wearing a kilt again, but with his white shirt and polished boots he's still almost elegant. Almost.

"Why are you looking like a cupcake?"

Crispin points at my dress without even trying to hide his laugh. I throw a ball of fire at him but he easily extinguishes it with a fountain of water before it reaches him.

"I do *not* look like a cupcake," I say with emphasis. Although he's right. He's absolutely right. It's the most hideous dress I've ever worn. It's fluffy pink skirt is too wide to let me walk unhindered through doors and the white ruffles around my chest hide my figure in the most unflattering way. It could work as fancy dress, but it's not something I want to wear in public.

"Are ye going to take it off?"

"You bet."

I'm already on the way to my wardrobe to look for something less... big. I choose a dark blue dress with a neckline decorated with sparkling crystals. It's comparatively comfy.

Suddenly, Storm is hugging me from behind.

"Do you need help getting out of this dress?" he whispers, already working on the buttons on my back. The seamstress didn't even add a zip, making him fumble with a long row of buttons instead. I'm going to kill her, slowly and with pleasure. While making her wear this cupcake abomination.

With every button he opens, he kisses the naked skin he exposes, slowly working his way down my back. I can't help but moan. When he's reached the end, just above my bum, he slides the dress down my shoulders. I'm not wearing a bra underneath, so I'm naked in front of him, my lace panties the only piece of clothing covering me from their views.

I know the other three are watching even before Storm turns me around. My nipples are hard and erect, aching to be touched. But Storm has other plans. He goes down on his knees and gently kisses me just below my belly button, before working his way down until he reaches my panties. He doesn't stop though, continuing on. The lace is so thin that it almost feels as if he's kissing my bare skin.

I feel myself getting wet and instinctively spread my legs to give him better access. He takes it as an invitation to push the panties to one side and run his tongue over my swollen flesh.

He holds my thighs as he enters me with his tongue, making me moan loudly.

I notice I've closed my eyes and open them only to see my other three Guardians watch me with desire. Arc has slipped a hand below his kilt and is stroking himself. Now I know what he wears beneath his kilt – nothing. They don't move closer, though, letting Storm be the one to bring me close to ecstasy.

He flicks his tongue over my bud before entering me with it, sucking hard and swallowing my wetness. I put my hands on his head, both to guide him to my sweet spot and to steady myself. I'm a mess, moaning and quivering, and then screaming when he makes me come.

Satisfied, he gets up and takes me into his arms, holding me tight as the last waves of the orgasm still run through me. Exhausted, I lean against his chest. It would be so nice to lie down on my bed now, with all four of my Guardians, having some more fun...

But that's when someone knocks on the door and I know that it's time to go.

With a sigh of regret, I step back.

"I need to clean myself up," I say hoarsely, starting to move towards the bathroom, but Storm grips my wrist and stops me.

"Don't. I want you to stay like you are. I want you to feel all evening that we will continue this later. That you came for me and are going to do it again tonight."

I shiver at his request, immediately feeling myself getting aroused again. These Guardians are going to be the death of me. Now I need to go to this ball, wet and horny, having to pretend I'm interested in what people are saying, doing small talk and probably dance with guests I don't know.

Being a Princess really isn't all it's made out to be.

To my disappointment, neither Thor nor Loki are attending the ball. Thor's daughter is here though, a human girl he adopted as a baby. She's surrounded by a swarm of male Guardians and it's no surprise. She's extremely pretty, especially for a human. I'd love to talk to her, but with all the guests vying for my attention, I doubt I'll get the chance.

My mother doesn't comment on my choice of dress, so she probably didn't know what the seamstress had planned for me. Again, I'm making murder plans. I don't know why that woman doesn't like me. I've been nothing but nice to her... except for the time I had to adapt one of her dresses because Crispin had cut holes into it. Maybe she's blaming me for that?

I really don't want to be thinking of dresses, but the wetness between my legs is a constant reminder that I'm naked beneath mine. I feel exposed, as if everyone can see what Storm did to me not long ago. I wish I could just leave and have him do it again and again in my bedroom.

Whenever I meet his gaze, he winks. And when I look at Arc, he raises an eyebrow suggestively. Did he come while watching me come? I didn't see but I'd love to know. Or if he's still hard beneath his kilt, waiting for relief...

"Lucifer, may I introduce you to my daughter, Wynter?"

My mother is suddenly by my side, a tall God next to her. He doesn't look like I imagined Lucifer. Of course I know he isn't the devil nor does he live in hell, but it's hard to get those thoughts out of my mind. Growing up on Earth has made me believe in some of the things humans do, and only now I am finding out how wrong they are.

Lucifer's black hair is pulled back into a ponytail, a stark contrast to his pristine white suit. His dark eyes are scrutinising me, making me want to turn away and hide. It's as if he can see into my soul and... No, those are human prejudices. He's just curious, wanting to meet the Queen's daughter.

"It's a pleasure to make your acquaintance." He smiles pleasantly before turning back to my mother.

"You must be so happy to have her back."

"I am indeed," my mother replies with a smile. She seems to like Lucifer. I wonder how he got his bad reputation on Earth. Does he have a doppelganger like Loki, who does all the bad stuff and then blames it on the original? Beira has told me how Jack, the God of Mischief, disguises himself as Loki whenever he travels to Earth. It's how Loki became known as a troublemaker, even though he's a sweet and gentle God, according to my mother. I'm really looking forward to meeting him, and Thor. Hopefully they'll be at the next ball.

"How are you finding the Winter Realm?" Lucifer asks me and I turn my attention back to the conversation.

"It's not as cold as I thought it would be. And what I've seen of the Realm so far, it's beautiful."

"It is, but of course it's no match for the fiery beauty of my own Realm." He smiles mischievously. "You should visit me sometime."

"I'm sure Wyn and her *Guardians* would love to visit," my mother replies with a smile, making it clear that I am already spoken for. Not that Lucifer is my type; he's far too old, despite his youthful look. Like with most of the Gods, it's his eyes that give away his true age. They are ancient and tell tales of a life full of both sorrow and happiness. Beira has told me how Lucifer likes to take human wives. He must have had hundreds of them over time, and it can't have been easy to watch them all die. I wonder why he does it when he knows that it will end in death. Why not be with a Guardian or God who will live forever?

"Guardians? Plural?" he asks curiously.

I shrug. "Why choose?"

Lucifer laughs heartily. "Well said, my lady. Bowing to convention is so boring."

"Are you here with someone?"

"Sadly not. I am without a partner currently, but I'm looking. If you know someone back on Earth, please let me know."

I think back to my girlfriends. None of them would make a good companion to a God, I think.

But I smile politely. "If I think of someone, I will certainly tell you."

"I'd appreciate it. I don't like spending more time on Earth than I need to. My reputation precedes me, if you know what I mean." He winks. "And now I must leave, your mother has asked me to do some research on a certain plant." He lowers his voice. "Congratulations on reaching Immortality, Princess. I will do my best to assist you in finding out who did this."

My heart warms at his sincere expression. It's good to see how my mother has loyal allies who care about what happens to her and her daughter.

"Thank you," I say and stretch out my hand to shake his, but he takes mine gently and presses a kiss on it. With a flourished bow, he takes his leave.

"He's quite the charmer," my mother chuckles as we watch him make his way through the crowd, giving small bows to most of the ladies he passes. "But he's a good man, and someone we're lucky to have on our side."

Taking the opportunity of having her all to myself, I ask her about the assassin.

"Did you manage to make him talk to you?"

My mother's expression darkens. "No, I did not. There's a spell on him, making it impossible for him to talk about it. I tried to lift it, but it's deeply embedded in his mind. If I removed it, it would likely break his mind and we wouldn't find out anything. The only solution I see at the moment is trying to gradually weaken the spell by working on it daily. I'm beginning to believe that he didn't do this willingly, so let's hope he wants to tell us. That will make it easier."

"Does that mean you will have to meet him daily?"

"No, luckily not. Ada should be strong enough to do it – she doesn't need to break the spell, just challenge it. She seems to be building up a rapport with the prisoner, so she might be the one he will confide in."

I clear my throat, preparing to ask the question that's been playing on my mind for days.

"Do you think they'll try again? If the dragon assassin was coerced into killing me, there must be others who will try?"

Beira smiles sadly. "There always are others. I've lost count of how often people have tried to kill me. But as you can see, I'm still alive, and so are you. Your Guardians are the best of the best and they would die to protect you. There are security measures in place that nobody knows about but me and a few select people, so don't worry. You're safe here. But I would ask you not to leave the Palace for now, until we know more."

As annoying as it is, I know she's right. Luckily, for what Arc and I are planning, we don't even need to leave my chambers. And besides that, I'm going to be busy with Council meetings and other official business. I'm meeting Tamara tomorrow so I can learn more about intelligence and how she gets her information. It's exciting; I've been wondering about that for a while. Tamara is a fascinating person and I'm looking forward to spending more time with her. While I love my Guardians, it's nice to talk to another woman from time to time. And I'm not sure my mother counts. She's a bit too... Goddess for that.

Chapter Thirteen

"**G**uys, get oot!"

I groan as Arc's loud voice wakes me. I'm snuggled between two men, warm and comfy, and I don't want them to leave. I draw the duvet over my head, hiding from the world. Noticing that I'm naked, I think back to last night and smile. We had fun, all five of us. No wonder I'm tired.

"Wyn, get up, we dinnae have much time. Yer mother has another meeting scheduled, so we need ta do it now."

I'm suddenly wide awake when I realise what he means. My parents. I'm finally going to see them again. Find out if they're alright. Maybe even persuade them to come live here in the Realm with me.

Crispin gives me a kiss on the cheek. "Good luck, little Princess."

"I'm not little!" I protest but he's already left the bed. Storm is the next to kiss me, but he chooses my lips. I want more than just his lips on mine and open my mouth, nudging his lips with my tongue. He responds in kind, kissing me passionately, but ends the kiss far too soon.

"Be good, Princess."

"When am I ever not good?"

He laughs. "Shall I remind you of last night?"

I blush, but Frost hugs me from behind.

"Don't worry, you were very good last night."

"Out!" Storm calls and they both jump out of bed, leaving me alone with my Scottish Guardian. Not that he's actually Scottish, but his accent and dress style certainly are. He reminds me of home. Most of the guys wearing kilts in Edinburgh do it for the tourists, but still, it's always a nice sight.

I sit up and the blanket slips down, giving Arc a nice view of my boobs.

"Put some clothes on or I won't be able ta focus," he growls and I laugh at his desperate look.

"Dinnae worry," I mock his accent and am promptly rewarded by having a pillow thrown at me.

I crawl out of bed and put on a silk kimono to hide most of my nakedness from Arc. My smooth legs are still visible though and he seems to have a hard time evading his eyes. Becoming a proper Demigoddess when I entered the Realms had the pleasant side effect that I no longer need to shave. It's saved me so much time, especially when having to wear dresses all the time.

"We need ta touch while doing this," Arc informs me and pats his lap. He's sat down in one of the large armchairs by the window, looking exceedingly comfy. I follow his invitation and lean against his broad chest, wiggling a little to find the best position.

"Dinnae distract me," he complains and I stop moving. "We need ta touch but we need ta concentrate as well."

"Okay, explain to me again how this is going to work."

"We're going ta connect with a demon who's currently in front of yer parents' hoose. If we're lucky. Demons aren't the most reliable people."

From the beginning, Beira had said that it would be too dangerous to send a Guardian there. After the Calanais battle, the Scotland Gate was only used for emergencies in the fear that demons might still be lying in wait on the other side.

So a demon is our only chance. Luckily, Arc knows a few that are amenable if the bribe is high enough. It's costing us a small fortune to get this one to do what we want, but being the Winter Heiress has its advantages. Access to the Royal coffers is one of them.

"I've only done this once before," Arc warns me. "It's not a nice feeling ta be in a demon's head. It's... slimy."

He checks his watch. "It's time. Ready?"

I nod. "Let's do this."

Without warning, everything goes black.

. . .

My parents' house looks surprisingly intact. Last time I saw it, the upper floor was on fire and the street was being shook by an earthquake. My earthquake, to be precise. Now, only a few thin lines on the wall tell of what happened. They've either had excellent builders at work or someone helped out with magic. I'm pretty sure it was the latter. You can't just restore an almost destroyed street back to how it was before in just a few weeks.

It feels strange looking out of the demon's eyes. We can't see him, just what he sees. He could be a hideous winged devil for all I know, but I'd hope that Arc has chosen one who can blend in. Or one who can do glamour magic. My parents have been traumatised enough, they don't need a demon on their doorstep.

Knock on the door, Arc commands inside the demon's head. Okay, now I really hope that the demon looks human.

We walk forward – well, the demon does, I'm just a passenger. It's a very surreal feeling. I can somehow feel his body, but only in a faint way, more an echo than an actual sensation. But his vision is as clear as if it was my own eyes.

The demon knocks once, twice. Nothing happens.

What's your name? I ask to bridge the tension.

Surprise fills the demons' mind.

Andrew, he finally answers.

I'm having a hard time hiding my laughter. A demon called Andrew? Seriously? That is the least demony name I could think of.

I can feel Arc's amusement through our link but hope it's not transmitted to the demon. We don't want to piss him off.

Finally, there are noises on the other side of the door and it slowly opens. My mother is looking straight at me. At the demon.

"Yes?" she asks tiredly. What time is it on Earth? Must be early morning, judging from her robe hastily thrown over her nightie.

She looks like she's been up all night. Her hair is tousled and there are shadows all around her eyes. She looks older than I remember. I hope it's just because she didn't sleep well and not because of ... well, me.

Tell her you're here on behalf of her daughter, Arc commands.

"I'm here on behalf of your daughter," Andrew repeats dutifully.

"My daughter isn't here. Please leave." Her expression darkens. She turns to close the door but Andrew puts his foot in the way.

"She's here with me through a mental link. She wants to talk to you."

My mum looks at him as if he's crazy. "Prove it," she challenges him and inside, I applaud her. Even though she's human, she's known about the supernatural world ever since she adopted me. She knew I wasn't human, but she accepted that.

Tell her that she drew me magic for my birthday.

He repeats it and my mum's eyes widen. "Tell me something else."

I rack my brain for something only she will know. When something comes to mind, I chuckle.

"She says she believed that haggis were real until she was in her early teens."

Mum smiles and opens the door. "Come on in."

Andrew follows her into our living room. On the way, she shouts up the staircase for my dad to come down quickly.

"Would you like some tea?" Oh how I love my mum. Offering tea to a demon. Not that she knows... but she'd probably do the same if she knew. That's just the way she is.

Andrew shakes his head, making me slightly dizzy.

A moment later, my dad enters the room, a bathrobe slung around his thin body. Just like my mum, he looks like he's not had much sleep recently. His face isn't as clean shaven as I'm used to either. What's going on with them?

"What's going on?"

"He's here for Wyn," mum tells him excitedly. "He's got a... mental link with her, he said?"

Andrew nods. "She's watching you right now. She can see and hear through me."

"Impossible," my father says with the frown usually reserved for his students.

"He knows things only Wyn would know," mum is quick to reassure him. "Let's hear him out."

With a sceptical grumble, dad sits down across from Andrew, scrutinising him.

Tell them that I miss them.

"She says she misses you."

Mum smiles. "Tell her we miss her too."

Are they alright?

"She wants to know if you are alright."

"A lot has happened since she left," my mother sighs. "There have been strange—"

"Don't tell him, he could be one of them," dad interrupts. "You may have convinced my wife, but you're yet to prove to me that Wyn is with you."

He adds vanilla to his pancakes. He always makes them for my birthday.

"You make vanilla pancakes for your daughter's birthday," Andrew says and my father's eyes widen.

"How much vanilla per pancake?"

One pinch of ground vanilla.

A smile spreads on my dad's face when Andrew repeats my words. Good, now that both of them are convinced that it's really me talking to them, we can start to talk properly.

Ask mum what she was going to say.

"We're being watched," my mum says before Andrew even has the chance to speak. "They follow us wherever we go. We've had phone calls where someone was whispering gibberish. And we've received these letters..."

Dad gets up and takes a stack of letters from the mantlepiece. He hands one of them to Andrew who slowly unfolds it.

WE'RE WATCHING YOU.

That's all it says but it makes a shiver run over my back.

My father gives Andrew a second letter.

SHE WILL KILL YOU.

Who is she? I ask no one in particular. I don't expect Andrew to know. Arc gives me a mental hug and I wish it was a real one.

Andrew reads a final letter.

INVITE WYNTER OR YOU WILL DIE.

"Of course, even if we'd known how to contact you, we wouldn't have asked you to visit," my mum hurries to say. "But you're not here in person so I'm sure they won't know it's you."

They're using my parents as bait. Anger boils up in me. Someone is threatening my parents just to get to me. That's unforgivable.

Ask them if they've ever seen one of the people watching them, Arc tells Andrew.

"At night, we sometimes see glowing eyes outside," mum says with a shudder. "They're all around the house, even in the garden. We no longer go outside after dark. At the beginning we called the police, but they never found anyone sneaking around. And nobody has ever tried to come into the house."

Andrew suddenly gets up.

"That's because we can't enter without being invited in."

He stretches out his hands and fiery ropes shoot towards my parents, wrapping around them, tying them up in seconds. They both scream in pain as the ropes burn their skin. I'm screaming too, shouting at Andrew to stop, to end this madness, but all he does is laugh as he watches my parents slump to the ground.

"Thanks for helping me, Princess. And now you better make your way to the Mistress before I accidentally kill the humans."

He laughs in disdain. My parents are writhing on the floor as blisters are forming on the skin. I'm crying, unable to see them in so much pain.

Stop it! I cry, begging him to stop.

"The Lady Morrigan sends her regards."

We're thrown out of his head and back into blackness.

"Call the Queen!" Arc shouts as soon as we open our eyes, back in my bedchamber. The guys must have been in their room next door because next thing I know, three concerned Guardians are crowding me, asking me whether everything is alright.

Of course it isn't.

My head is spinning. This can't be happening. This isn't real.

I curl up on the floor, my parents' anguished faces flashing through my mind. Their pain, so much pain. Their blistered skin, the rope hurting them. The laugh of the demon who tricked us all.

"It was a trap... The demon used us to get into the house... He kidnapped her parents..."

Their words drift past me, but I can't seem to focus on them.

My dad.

Mum.

Their pain.

Their wounds.

I failed them.

It's all my fault.

I pull my legs close to my chest, making myself small. Maybe it's all just a dream. Maybe they're safe at home. Maybe...

Cool air touches my tear-streaked cheeks.

"Wyn?"

I look up at my mother. Beira. My birth mother who didn't help my real parents. She just left them on Earth to fend for themselves. They are humans so they don't matter to her. All that matters to her is herself. She's selfish, cruel, cold.

Just as cold as the air on my cheek.

My magic pours out of me, fiery hot, ready to burn and destroy. I let it, I don't care any longer. The magic takes control, relishing in its new freedom. It races through the room, setting things on fire. I can smell burning, but I stay on the floor.

"Wyn, stop it!"

People are shouting. Who cares. My parents are hurt. Maybe dead.

Cold water douses me and I shriek in shock. Someone puts his hands on my cheeks, lifting me up to look at him.

"Wyn, you need to stop."

It's Frost. His expression is a strange one. Fear? Of me? Or of the flames surrounding me. Then I remember. His element is water. He doesn't like fire. I burned him before.

Oh no, I can't hurt my Guardian. I pull at my magic, trying to reign it in but it's too wild. Too violent.

"I can't," I whisper and his eyes soften.

"Yes, you can. Change your magic to water. Feel around you. Feel the snow outside, full of water you can use. I can douse the flames but they keep returning. You need to shut them off for good."

I reach out for my water magic. It's no use. The fire is too strong. My magic is pouncing, her claws outstretched whenever I try and approach.

"She's too strong." I can feel myself grow weaker, the magic taking all my strength. I should have trained her better. I should have done those lessons with my Guardians as intended. But there were always other things to do. I never got the chance. And now she's feral and doing what she wants.

"Wyn, listen to me. Focus on water…"

Suddenly, his lips are on mine and he kisses me wildly, nudging me to respond. I open my mouth and he enters me with his tongue. He feels cool and calming. Wet. Water. I can feel his magic inside of him, a cold lake ready to be used. I draw on it and channel it into myself, dousing my magic in it. She shrieks and fights the water that is threatening her fire, but with Frost's power, I'm finally strong enough.

I feel for the water in the snow outside, that endless resource of water, and suck it in, channelling it through myself and then out into the room. Smoke fills the air as the fire is extinguished.

But all I want to feel is Frost's mouth on mine, our kiss, our desperation, like two people drowning. I cling to my Guardian as the last of the fires die off.

With the fire gone, tiredness claims me. I'm too weak to even continue the kiss. I sink against Frost's chest and he embraces me, holding me close.

"Rest, Princess."

"Will you stay?" I whisper weakly and he runs his hands over my back in response.

"Of course. I will be here until you wake up again."

I smile and sink into the darkness waiting for me.

Chapter Fourteen

At first, everything is good. I'm in Frost's arms, my head on his chest. I know it's him because he smells of sea salt and waves. I'm warm and comfy. Safe. His breaths are deep and regular but too fast for him to be sleeping. If he knows that I'm awake, he doesn't show it.

I could let the sound of his breathing let me lull back to sleep.

Then I remember what happened. Mum. Dad.

I sit up and jump out of bed. I need to save them.

"Wyn, wait!"

Frost is climbing out of my four-poster bed, looking tired. Did he stay awake while I was sleeping?

Wait, that's not my bed. This isn't my room. It looks like one of the guest rooms, decorated in the generic Palace style.

I must have damaged my own chambers so much that they're no longer inhabitable. I should feel guilty, but all I feel is a gaping darkness inside my chest, telling me to take revenge. To burn and to kill my way to the Morrigan who took my parents from me.

I storm out of the room and into a corridor I don't recognise.

"At least put on some clothes!" Frost shouts and I look down at me. I'm wearing a large nightshirt, but nothing besides that.

I couldn't care less.

I turn right, hoping that this will get me out of the guest wing. My bare feet are almost silent on the marble floor as I run away from Frost. I need to see Beira. I need her to tell me that everything is going to be alright. That she has a solution. A way to get my parents back.

At the end of the corridor, I find a familiar courtyard. I know where I am now. I enter the tower on the other side of the courtyard and shout, "Fifth floor, fast!" as soon as I reach the first step of the staircase.

The stairs begin to turn, quickly becoming faster, transporting me upwards. Usually I avoid this speed on the way up because it makes me dizzy, but not today.

When the staircase comes to a stop on the fifth floor, I run through my mother's vestibule and into her private study. It's empty. A hidden door behind one of the wooden bookshelves brings me into a narrow passage leading to her bedchambers. Again, empty. I curse. I should have asked Frost instead of running away like a headless haggis.

Luckily, a breathless Frost arrives.

"They're in the Council Chambers," he huffs. How is he so out of breath? Did I run that fast?

"But you need to slow down, Wyn. Your magic is sparking again."

I raise my arms. Indeed, there are fiery little sparks floating on my skin, sizzling slightly as if they could turn into lightning any second now. I reach down into my heart cave and soothe my magic. She's agitated, but not as violent as she was when I set my room on fire. I think she's just as scared as I am.

I whisper to her and the sparks disappear.

"Now look at me," Frost says soothingly and grips my shoulders tightly, grounding me. I look into his dark, intense eyes. "Breathe."

I hadn't noticed I was breathing rapidly. My whole body is not feeling like it's supposed to. Like it's not really mine.

"In... and out...."

I do as Frost tells me to, breathing with him, slowly becoming calmer.

"In.... out..."

His gaze holds me locked in place and I can't help but continue to look at him. My Frost.

"I'm sorry," I whisper.

"There's nothing to be sorry for. I would have probably flooded the entire Palace by now." He chuckles. "But you can't appear in the Council like this. It would do more harm than good."

He opens my mother's wardrobe and randomly chooses a dress.

"Put this on. Poor Algonquin would probably get a heart attack if he sees the Princess in a nightie."

Despite the emptiness inside of me, I have to smile. I slip into the dress and even smooth my hair in front of the mirror. Now I look a lot less crazy than I must have before.

"Ready?" Frost asks me gently and I give him a tight nod.

"Thanks."

He smiles. "Anytime."

The entire Council is in attendance when we arrive. They all rise as we enter, even Beira.

"I'm so sorry, my lady," Gwain says sadly and the others in the room grumble their agreement. Ada gives me a quick hug before I sit down by my mother's side. I ignore her. I can't bear to look at her just now.

Storm is sitting on his usual place on my left. Surprisingly, Arc and Crispin are also sitting on the table this time instead of standing in the background. But it makes sense, at least for Arc. He was there when it all happened.

"How are you feeling?" my mother asks quietly.

"Do you know where they are?" I ask instead, ignoring her question. I wouldn't know what to say anyway. My heart is in uproar and I'm having trouble keeping my magic in check.

"No. We found the last known location of the Morrigan abandoned." Tamara surprises me by speaking up. Only now do I notice that she's sitting next to Zephyr. Looks like all convention is being thrown aside today.

"We've sent Guardians to their house, but of course nobody was there," the spymistress reports. "They've split into teams and are now travelling to the nearest Gates, seeing if they can find any traces. But if it's really the Morrigan who's pulling all the strings, it's likely she won't need to use Gates to transport them to wherever she's hiding."

"What does she want with them?" I ask. "Is it just because she wants me to come to her?"

"Either that, or to show us that it's all been her doing. She's finally creeping out of the shadows and is showing that she's been pulling the strings all along."

"But what about Angus?"

"Oh, I'm sure some of it was him," my mother says dismissively. "The attack on you on that ferry, the kidnapping before, those sound like Angus. And the assassination attempt on me, perhaps. But the dragon shifter being sent to kill you, but not willingly... that's not like him at all."

"And the Morrigan would be strong enough to put that spell on him," Arc adds. "From what I've heard of her, mind manipulation is her speciality."

I think of Crispin and how she manipulated him into serving her for so long and can't help but shudder. And that monster now has my parents.

"Why don't you keep track of your Gods?" I ask my mother, not even trying to hide the accusation in my voice.

"I know where most of them are, but some, like the Morrigan, are extremely good at hiding. Especially after I expelled her from her own Realm... nobody had heard from her in decades. Until now."

"You should have killed her back then. After what she did..." I look at Crispin but it's clear he doesn't want me to mention him. Maybe not everybody knows that he was once the Morrigan's slave.

"I can't kill my creations," Beira sighs. "It's one of the universal laws that I cannot kill what I created in the first place. It would rebound on me and kill me as well. I had planned to imprison the Morrigan but she escaped before she could be captured."

"Couldn't someone else have killed her?" I ask, ignoring that I'm likely sounding extremely insolent and whiny.

My mother is silent for a moment. I can't stand it any longer.

"Tell us!" I shout, jumping up. Sparks are flying all around me once again and Storm puts a hand on my arm, slowly pulling me back down on my chair.

"She's too strong," Beira says quietly. "I created her to be my first in command. My successor, even. When Angus started to fight the natural order of Winter and Summer, I felt like I needed someone who could fight the coming wars for me, someone more ruthless and callous than me. So I created the Morrigan, the Goddess of War and Violence. I poured more strength into her than into any other God before. She has the power of three Gods, something I felt was important for a protectress of my Realm. But she was never interested in fighting wars to protect. All she wanted was death and destruction. After the last big war with Angus, I gave the Morrigan her own Realm to keep her out of trouble. I should have known that it wouldn't work."

I'm stunned. "Why would you create a Goddess so powerful that you couldn't control her?"

"It was the only way to keep my Realm safe. My people needed someone to fight for them."

It's easy to read between the lines. She's not infallible. Just because she's the Mother of Gods doesn't mean that she can't make mistakes.

But this mistake may have cost me everything.

"I've sent messengers into all the Realms, warning our allies," Gwain says into the silence, tactfully interrupting our conversation. "If one of them knows of the Morrigan's whereabouts, we will find out soon."

Zephyr clears his throat. "The Dragon ambassador still hasn't replied. I'm worried their Realm might be affected by the Morrigan as well. It's not like him to ignore my messages."

"It looks like she's been planning this for a long time," my mother says with conviction. "We have been blind, too focussed on Angus and his open threat to see the Morrigan closing in. But it's not too late. Whatever she's planning, we're stronger. We have allies – we may have chosen them to fight against Angus if necessary, but they will stand with us against the Morrigan as well. She may be the bigger threat for now. I much prefer an enemy that I can see rather than one lurking in the shadows."

"But what about my parents?" I'm having trouble not to shout again. As much as I understand that we have to talk about the wider consequences, what really matters right now is my mum and dad. I try and push away the memories of their bloodied bodies, but they flash in front of my eyes nonetheless.

Storm squeezes my hand in reassurance. I'm grateful that I have all my Guardians in this room; I couldn't guarantee that I wouldn't run amok again otherwise.

"We can't do anything until we know where the Morrigan is hiding," Gwain says gently. "But I imagine she will be in touch soon. She's taken them for a reason, most likely as hostages. And a hostage doesn't make sense without demands. I'm surprised the demon didn't tell you directly what she wanted from you."

"That traitor," Arc spats.

"How did you find him?" my mother asks him and a guilty look draws over his face.

"He's one of Aodh's rehabilitated demons. Aodh and his demon partner Chesca took in some demons instead of killing them and tried to change their nature. It worked in some cases. In others, the demons had to be killed in the end. But this one... he came highly recommended, a model convert. I would never have expected him to turn on us."

"We will have a talk about that in the future, Guardian," my mother says sternly and Arc's shoulders fall.

I'm beginning to think that Beira didn't know all the details of our plan. At least not the fact that it involved a demon. As much as I want to blame him, I can't. It was me who pressured him into it. I wanted to see them.

It's my fault.

There's noise outside the Council Chambers and a moment later, someone knocks. That can't mean anything good. The Lord Chamberlain is usually waiting outside, not letting anyone in.

My heart sinks as Jonathan enters the room, followed by a servant carrying a large metal box.

"Your Highnesses, I'm sorry for the interruption, but this was delivered to the Palace Gates just moments ago. The man delivering it... he took poison the moment we'd taken the box of him."

Gwain gets up and takes the box.

"Thanks, Jonathan. Dismissed."

The Lord Chamberlain seems a little miffed that he has to leave, but he follows Gwain's command. We sit in silence as the Master of Arms puts the box onto the table in front of him.

He lays his hands onto the lid and closes his eyes in concentration. He looks relieved when he opens them again.

"I can't feel any magical traps or threats. No signs of life either. Still, we should proceed with caution. The box should never have been brought here. I recommend your Highnesses leave until we know what is in there."

My mother sighs in irritation and with a flick of her hand, we're all behind a glistening barrier, with the exception of Gwain.

"There you go, we're all protected. Now open that box before I do it myself."

Gwain looks like he's about to protest, but then decides not to. He's been around Beira long enough to know that she always gets what she wants. Even if, like in my case, it takes her twenty-two years.

He carefully lifts the lid on the side closest to him and peeks inside.

"Oh no."

His face is a mask of horror as he closes the lid again.

"Your Majesty, I recommend that the Princess is not to look at this."

I jump up in fury and walk towards the box.

"The Princess is going to do exactly that." I push him aside and ignore his protests. He's far too loyal to the Crown to put his hands on me.

"Wyn, don't," my mother warns, but I'm not listening. I open the box... and scream.

It can't be... No. Please, no.

I stagger back, stumbling into Storm's waiting arms.

"No, no, no," is all I can whisper as the reality of what I just saw sinks in.

I need to see it again. I need to make sure.

I push out of Storm's embrace and open the box again. This time, I see a small note attached to the content.

Touch me.

As if in trance, I reach out and touch the bloody hand lying on a red cushion inside the box.

My mother's hand.

"What are they going to do to us, James?" she asks, but he doesn't have any answers either. They arrived in this *dark place not long ago, but neither knows how long they were unconscious for.*

The nice-looking man in the suit who was speaking on Wyn's behalf suddenly had ropes that burned. Rose rubs her arms, still hurting. Thick red welts have formed all over their bodies, but right now, she's more concerned about her daughter.

Wyn had been gone for weeks with no word whether she had managed to reach her mother. Rose grimaces at that thought. She's Wyn's mother, not that Goddess. She's raised her for twenty-two years, she's held Wyn when she was sad, she taught her how to walk and talk, she worried when Wyn was experimenting with her magic. And James, of course.

When the suited man arrived and he could prove that Wyn was with him somehow, Rose was overjoyed. She was worried, of course, that the stalkers would find out, but that didn't matter then. Talking to her daughter was the only thing that mattered.

She shakes her head. Her mind is sluggish, somehow, and it's hard to think. The darkness around them doesn't help either. She can't even see the floor she's sitting on. Nor can she see James, but she knows he's here with her. She's tried to get to him but there's something between them; glass, maybe.

"Whatever they do, let's just be glad they don't have Wyn," James says softly and she nods. Yes, as long as Wyn is safe, it doesn't matter.

Suddenly, someone is next to her.

"We need to send Wyn a message," a high-pitched voice says close to Rose's ear. "Do you volunteer to be the messenger?"

"No, I will do it!" James shouts from afar, but all Rose can think of is seeing Wyn again.

"Yes," she whispers and the voice next to her cackles.

"Good girl."

Something glints through the darkness, something metal.

At first, she feels no pain.

Then it overwhelms her.

Warm blood runs from where her arm was a moment ago. Then another pain, in her heart. For a second, she can see the rod of metal sticking out of her chest.

James screaming in the distance is the last thing she hears before death claims her.

Chapter Fifteen

When I resurface from the memory, I'm on the floor. Beira's holding me in her arms, her eyes filled with worry. So unlike her.

"What happened?" she asks. Of course, she doesn't know. For them, it's just a hand. A bloody hand where you can see the bone sticking out on one end. But the tattoo around the wrist gives it away. A bracelet of delicate hearts that mum got tattooed when she adopted me. There's no doubt that it's her. Even without the tattoo, the thick red marks on her skin tell of the fiery rope she was bound with.

"She's dead," I whisper, my words making it even more real.

"Are you sure?" Gwain asks from behind my mother. "They could have... taken the hand while she was still alive."

"She's dead," I repeat. "I saw it, I felt it."

"But why?" Gwain starts walking up and down the room. "There was no demand, no threat. Why kill a hostage without warning?"

I hate how logical he's thinking. Why isn't everyone crying along with me. Wait. Am I crying? I gingerly touch my cheeks. No tears.

I'm not crying over my mum's death.

I should be a wreck, crying my eyes out, but instead, I get up and look at the arm again. I'm cold, clinical. Ice is starting to rise up in me, covering my heart. It's necessary. I need to rise up to be the person I was born to be.

The Winter Heiress.

Cold. Emotionless. A true ruler.

I get up and one last time, I confirm what I already know. Yes, it's my mum's hand. She's dead.

Next step.

"Search the man who brought this here," I tell Ada. "Maybe he had a message for us that the guards didn't see."

"Princess..." she starts but one cold look from me shuts her up. She gives me a sharp salute and leaves.

"Gwain, retrace the man's route. If he's come from the Morrigan, maybe we can find her through him."

I know that chance is miniscule, the Goddess of War would know better. But no matter how small the chance, we still need to find out.

"Yes, ma'am." The old Guardian salutes me, but his expression is one of sadness. He knows things have changed. And he also knows they'll never be as they were before.

I feel the ice harden around my heart as I turn to my Guardians. I hate what I'm about to do.

"Crispin, write down all you know about the Morrigan. Any weaknesses, any strengths you think are important. Then write down what you think isn't important."

It's going to hurt. He's not ready yet to put his past into words. He just about managed to show me. But for him to actually write about it, word by word... it's going to break him. The cracks in his soul will widen and break and it will be my task to put him back together again. If I am still able to by then.

I am getting colder by the minute. The bond I feel with my Guardians is slowly freezing. I can't think of them as mine. They are tools that I need to use to find the Morrigan. And then to kill her. Only once that is done can I let my heart thaw again.

By then, it might be too late for us.

"Wynter, you need to stop."

My mother is looking at me strangely, almost as if she's worried. She should be proud of me right now. I'm trying to be like her. It's killing me inside but it's necessary. She's herself is the best example that it's possible to shut out the world, to be cold to everyone around you.

"Arc. If it was the Morrigan who put the spell on the dragon's mind, can you somehow follow it back? Find out more about her and why she did it?"

"I dinnae think so and it could hurt the prisoner, but..."

"Do it. I don't care if it hurts him."

I turn to Storm, but before I can say something, he speaks.

"Wyn, you are not yourself right now. You've just lost your mother, you're grieving." He takes a step towards me but I instinctively move away from him. I don't want him to get too close. He sighs as he notices that I'm not going to fall into his arms as he'd probably hoped. "You just told Arc to hurt a prisoner. That's not you. You need to take a break, you—"

"And what good will that do?" I snarl, frustrated that he can't see the idiocy of his request. "She has my father, she is threatening us all. We need to do something now, not later. There is no time to rest. We still don't know what she wants. There is so much to do, why can't you see that?!" I shout the last sentence, shocking the room into silence.

I ignore them all and walk out of the room, then break into a run. I can't be inside, I need air. I run up the stairs, ignoring the magic that could transport me up a lot quicker than my legs can. There are people following me, probably my Guardians, but I don't wait for them.

When I reach the top of the tower, I don't stop running and jump into the air, my wings expanding immediately. I fly, soaring on the icy wind, driving all thoughts and emotions from my mind. All I can feel is the elation of the flight, the cold wind on my cheeks, the little ice crystals forming on my skin.

I fold my wings close to my back and dive down, towards the snowy landscape before. There are some moving shapes below, snow hares maybe?

I follow them as they race over the frozen ground. Yes, it's hares, jumping fast from one snow drift to the next. I watch them, amazed at their speed and agility. They're so free...

Suddenly, there's a tree in front of me and I swerve to the side, almost crashing into it. Watch where you're flying, Wyn. I can't believe I let myself be distracted by bunnies. But at least I managed to think of something else than death and destruction. The cold air has helped clear my head a little.

I manage to land, not very elegantly but at least I didn't fall. This place looks familiar. That tree...

Oh no.

"Are you here for more sparklies?" Blaze's melodious voice makes me swirl around. The unicorn is blending into the white landscape around us, its silver fur shimmering in the sun.

"Yes. I think I am." I offer him a grim smile. "Give me the strongest stuff you've got."

Epilogue
Chesca

The guards are just as surprised as me when I stumble through the Gate into the Winter Realm. I never thought it would let me through. It's unheard of for a demon to travel to one of the Realms of the Gods. Especially not Beira's.

But I'm here now and the guards are beginning to gather their wits. Weapons are pointing at me and one Guardian steps forward, his hands extended. Something grabs me from behind, pressing my hands and wings against my body, but when I look, there is nothing. Magic.

"I come in peace!" I shout and the guards look even more confused. "I have an urgent message for your Queen."

And her daughter. Wyn. But I assume that Beira will be the one who's still responsible for what happens in her Realm. I can't imagine Wyn being concerned with any of that. Even when she was about to head into battle at Calanais, all she had eyes for were her Guardians.

"What would a demon have to say to the Mother of Gods?" the Guardian at the front of the crowd shouts. I don't know much about the Queen's military, but I'm sure the golden stripes on his shoulders mean he's important.

"I say we kill her now," a scarred soldier next to him says loud enough for me to hear. "She'll only attack her Majesty as soon as she has a chance."

"I know who sent the demons who attacked the Gate at Calanais and who tried to kill Princess Wynter and her Guardians!"

That makes them listen.

"Because you're one of them?" the Guardian in charge sneers and I laugh.

"No, because I killed most of them. Now let me speak to Beira."

Some of the soldiers gasp in shock. I sigh.

"I mean her Majesty."

"She doesn't have any respect," the scarred man snarls, his eyes filled with hate. "If you won't, I'll kill her. You know what demons did to my family."

"Stand down, soldier," the leader commands icily. "Nathan, inform the Queen that we have a demon in custody."

A lanky blond Guardian runs to one of the huts to the right of the Gate and disappears inside.

"What's your name, demon?" the man in charge asks me.

"I am Chesca, Demon Queen of the Topaz Zone in the Demon Realm." I say my name with pride. I don't often get the opportunity to use my title and usually avoid it when talking to other demons. I've been in exile for centuries and haven't been to Topaz for just as long. And with the Morrigan taking over the Realm, I'm not even sure if my queendom is still like it was when I left.

"I didn't know demons had queens," one of the soldiers mutters. "Maybe she's lying to make herself sound important."

"No, Topaz exists alright." The scarred man approaches me. There is nothing but hate in the look he's giving me. "Do you know a Cristian?"

I freeze. I haven't heard that name in a long time. Not since I left and he tried to force me to return.

"Yes," I say slowly. "He's my brother."

The man comes closer.

"Stand down, Kahol!" the commander shouts.

"Just checking her for weapons, Sir," Kahol replies with a short salute and walks around me until he's standing behind me. I can feel his breath on my neck as his hands roam over my back.

"Cristian slaughtered my wife," he whispers so only I can hear. I'm beginning to struggle against the invisible bonds holding me in place. This man is deranged, he won't listen to his commander. He's out for revenge. "He raped my daughter before killing her. He almost managed to kill me. See the scars on my face?"

He steps in front of me and begins to pat me down.

"He made those. I could have had them healed, but I wanted a reminder of what he did to my family. And now I've got his sister standing in front of me."

"I hate him just as much as you," I whisper frantically. "He—"

He punches me in the stomach before I can continue. I gasp for breath, struggling for air.

The other soldiers are watching dispassionately. Their commander has disappeared, he's probably in one of the huts. But his bonds are still holding me in place. I can't escape.

Kahol steps behind me once more and I feel something sharp against my back.

"I wish it was him instead of you, but you will do."

Without further warning, he slams the dagger into my chest. Bones crunch and I know it pierces my heart before I feel the pain.

Blood fills my mouth and my vision is getting blurry.

But I need to pass on my message.

Need to.

"It's... the Morrigan. Tell... the Queen... the Morrigan controls... demons."

Death is close.

"They're... coming."

It's not over yet. This story continues in <u>Winter Queen</u>.

Subscribe to my newsletter to get regular news about my books: **skyemackinnon.com/newsletter**

If you enjoyed Winter Heiress, please consider leaving a review.

Author's Note

I hope you enjoyed reading this book! It was a lot of fun to write; Wyn is one of my favourite characters ever who keeps surprising me.

If you're wondering what happened to Chesca between the end of Winter Princess and Winter Heiress, you can find out in <u>Demon's Revenge</u>, a spin-off available to read for free.

There's also a prequel to Winter Princess called Mother of Gods, telling the love story between Beira and Colan.

Set in another universe, but no less magical is the dystopian reverse harem Rescued by Them featuring some very sexy bear shifters (including a polar bear!).

Or try Song of Souls, a fantasy novel with a tortured hero and an enemies to lovers romance.

Happy reading!

Skye MacKinnon

About the Author

Skye MacKinnon is a Scottish romance author who was raised by elves in the mystical Highlands and calls the Loch Ness monster her friend. Her bestselling books weave together romance with action, suspense and whimsical humour, creating page-turners filled with strong heroines, alpha heroes and loveable monsters.

Whether she's writing about aliens in kilts, hunky Vikings or cat shifter assassins, Skye likes to put a new spin on familiar tropes. Some of her heroines don't have to choose, some fall in love with other women, and others get abducted by clueless aliens.

Skye lives with her bossy cat on the west coast of Scotland and uses the dramatic views from her office as an inspiration, no matter whether she writes fantasy, paranormal or science fiction romance. Until she gets abducted by aliens, that is.

Subscribe to her newsletter:
skyemackinnon.com/newsletter

Also by Skye MacKinnon

Find all of Skye's books on her website, **skyemackinnon.com**, where you can also order signed paperbacks and swag. Many of her books are available as audiobooks.

Paranormal & Fantasy Romance

- **Claiming Her Bears** (post-apocalyptic shifter reverse harem)
- **Daughter of Winter** (fantasy reverse harem)
- **Catnip Assassins** (urban fantasy reverse harem)
- **Infernal Descent** (paranormal reverse harem based on Dante's Inferno, co-written with Bea Paige)
- **Seven Wardens** (fantasy reverse harem co-written with Laura Greenwood)
- **The Lost Siren** (post-apocalyptic, paranormal reverse harem co-written with Liza Street)

Science Fiction Romance

- **Starlight Highlanders Mail Order Brides** (sci-fi m/f romance, part of the Intergalactic Dating Agency)

- **Starlight Vikings** (sci-fi m/f romance, part of the Intergalactic Dating Agency)
- **Starlight Mermen** (sci-fi m/f romance, part of the Intergalactic Dating Agency)
- **Starlight Monsters** (m/f romance)
- **The Intergalactic Guide to Humans** (sci-fi romance with various pairings)
- **Between Rebels** (sci-fi reverse harem set in the Planet Athion shared world)
- **The Mars Diaries** (sci-fi reverse harem)
- **Through the Gates** (dystopian reverse harem co-written with Rebecca Royce)
- **Aliens and Animals** (f/f sci-fi romance co-written with Arizona Tape)

Other Series

- **Academy of Time** (time travel academy standalones, reverse harem and m/f)
- **Defiance** (contemporary reverse harem with a hint of thriller/suspense)

Standalones

- Song of Souls – m/f fantasy romance, fairy tale retelling
- Wings of Time and Fate - YA fantasy
- Highland Butterflies – lesbian romance

Box Sets

- Daggers & Destiny – a Skye MacKinnon starter library
- Stars & Seduction - a Sci-Fi Romance starter library